JB
CKN

D0597263

Knute Rockne

Young Athlete

Illustrated by Robert Doremus

Knute Rockne

Young Athlete

By Guernsey Van Riper, Jr.

Aladdin Paperbacks

CEDAR PARK PUBLIC LIBRARY
550 DISCOVERY BLVD.
CEDAR PARK, TEXAS 78613
(512) 259-5353

If you purchased this book without a cover you should be aware that this book is stolen property. It was reported as "unsold and destroyed" to the publisher and neither the author nor the publisher has received any payment for this "stripped book."

Aladdin Paperbacks
An imprint of Simon & Schuster
Children's Publishing Division
1230 Avenue of the Americas
New York, NY 10020
Copyright © 1952, 1959 by the Bobbs-Merrill Co., Inc.
All rights reserved including the right of reproduction
in whole or in part in any form.

First Aladdin Paperbacks edition, 1986
Printed in the United States of America

15 14 13 12 11 10 9 8
Library of Congress Cataloging-in-Publication Data

Van Riper, Guernsey, 1909–
  Knute Rockne, young athlete.

  Reprint. Originally published: Indianapolis: Bobbs-
Merrill, c1959.
  Summary: A biography focusing on the childhood of
the legendary football coach at Notre Dame, who won fame
for his insistence on good sportsmanship and his football
strategy.
  1. Rockne, Knute, 1888–1931—Juvenile literature.
2. Football—United States—Coaches—Biography—
Juvenile literature.   3. University of Notre Dame—
Football—Juvenile literature.   [1. Rockne, Knute, 1888–
1931.   2. Football—Coaches]   I. Doremus, Robert, ill.
II. Title.
GV939.R6V36   1986   796.332'092'4 [B] [92]   86-10791
ISBN 0-02-042110-9

Illustrations

Full pages

Numerous smaller illustrations

Contents

Books by Guernsey Van Riper, Jr.

BABE RUTH: ONE OF BASEBALL'S GREATEST

JIM THORPE: INDIAN ATHLETE

KNUTE ROCKNE: YOUNG ATHLETE

LOU GEHRIG: ONE OF BASEBALL'S GREATEST

RICHARD BYRD: BOY OF THE SOUTH POLE

WILL ROGERS: YOUNG COWBOY

★ ★ # Knute

Rockne

Young Athlete

Knute Takes
a Dare

"HURRY, ANNE!" The small, blond boy dashed into the cold lake water with a great splash. He swam about and kicked and thrashed. Soon he began to feel warm.

"Come in, Anne!" he called.

On the shore, his older sister finally finished undressing. She plunged in. "Oooh, it feels like ice!" she gasped.

"No, it feels good! I'm going to swim to the island today."

"Knute Rockne, you can't!" Anne stood up in the shallow water. "You're only four years old."

"I know I can," said Knute, stubbornly. Ever

since he had learned to swim, this summer of 1892, he had looked forward to this day. It was fun to paddle about in the cool water of the lake, far up in the Voss Mountains of Norway. But he was tired of just paddling.

"Ma told me to look after you. And you shouldn't try to swim that far! You'll get a cramp!"

"You can't stop me." Before Anne could say another word, Knute started for the island.

"Knute, come back here!" Anne kept calling. But he paid no attention. He swam right on.

"Oh, Knute!" said Anne sadly. Her face was worried as she stood watching. She was only six, but Ma had told her always to take care of her little brother.

Knute was thinking, "I'll fool Anne!" He took a deep breath and dived under the surface. He swam underwater until his lungs felt as though they would burst.

12

Anne was sure he had drowned. She looked
around desperately for help. There was no one
in sight.

Finally Knute had to come to the surface. He
gasped for air, rolled over on his back and waved.

"Oh, you're naughty!" Anne stamped her foot so hard she slipped and splashed full length in the shallow water. When she got up, Knute was again swimming straight toward the island.

In a few minutes he crawled out on a grassy bank. He scrambled up, panting, and sat down on a rock to catch his breath and look about. All around the lake were mountain peaks still capped with snow, even in late August. Knute started around the island. It was so tiny he soon circled it. So he plunged in to swim back.

Halfway, his arms and legs began to feel heavy. "Anne was right," he thought. "The island *is* a long way from the shore." It hurt his chest to breathe, and he grew a little frightened. He thrashed harder with his arms and legs, but only got more tired. He'd have to rest.

He rolled on his back and floated for a while. Soon it seemed easier to breathe. Then he struck out with the long steady strokes he had learned

14

from his friend, Olaf Larson. This was better! In a few minutes he reached shallow water. Then he waded out on the shore.

"I did it!"

Anne was already dressed. She tossed her head and looked the other way.

"I was only teasing you," said Knute. But still Anne wouldn't answer. He felt bad. He walked over to put on the sweater he had left on the ground. But he was still too wet. He would have to run about to dry off.

Behind the scrubby pine trees that dotted the shore, he caught sight of some blue mountain flowers. They grew right up against a snowbank. He ran to pick a bunch of them. He was grinning as he darted back and handed them to Anne. "Here—aren't they pretty?"

Anne took them without a word. Then she giggled. "Oh, Knute, they *are* pretty! But you were naughty."

15

Knute shook his head. "Olaf swims to the island," he argued. He pulled on his clothes.

Anne couldn't think of any answer. "We must take our berries to Ma," she said. The children picked up their buckets of yellow cloudberries they had picked before their swim. They both hurried along the shore.

They climbed to the top of a small rocky hill. Ahead of them was a *saeter*, one of the many Norwegian summer farms where butter and cheese were made. The *saeter* was only a meadow and a cottage, but it was a good place to bring cows to graze. And it was a pleasant place for the Rocknes to spend the summer!

Their mother sat in front of the low wooden house, knitting. On the ground at her feet, their baby sister Martha played with her doll. In the meadow beyond were four brown cows.

"There comes Olaf," said Knute. "That means it's milking time!"

16

A dark-haired twelve-year-old boy appeared at the far end of the pasture. Olaf Larson lived on the winter farm down in the valley.

Knute broke into a run. He set his bucket of berries down by the house, picked up a stick and ran on to the meadow.

"Come on! Come o-on!" he called. The cows lifted their heads and chewed their cuds. Knute rapped them smartly with the stick. They mooed and started lazily toward the house.

Mrs. Rockne and Anne got the pails and stool ready. Mrs. Rockne began to milk the cows.

"*Goddag!* Good day!" cried Olaf. "I've brought you fish and bread."

Knute couldn't wait to tell his news. "I swam to the island today, Olaf!"

Mrs. Rockne stopped milking. "Knute," she said, "I've told you to be careful!"

Anne told just what Knute had done. Mrs. Rockne sighed.

17

"Why, that isn't so far to swim," said Olaf.

Anne said, "You're much older and bigger than Knute. It was harder for him than it would be for you."

"But, Ma," Knute said, "I *knew* I could swim that far. I practiced along the shore."

"I never knew such an active boy! Why must you be so restless?"

"Well, I like to swim. And I wanted to reach the island before we go home."

"We are going back to town next week," Mrs. Rockne said. "It will soon be too cold for swimming. And Anne will have to start to school."

Anne brought a package from the house. "Here's the cheese we made yesterday, Olaf."

Olaf took it. "Wish I could stay for a swim," he said, "but my father told me to bring the cheese right back today."

"Come earlier tomorrow," Mrs. Rockne suggested. "Good-by!"

18

"Good-by!" called the children as Olaf went off across the meadow.

"And now, young man," Mrs. Rockne said, "I know you're eager to swim and climb and run— but I don't want you to be foolish and reckless."

Knute was puzzled. "How will I know whether I'm foolish? Pa always told me, 'Learn to do a thing perfectly, and you'll be all right.' And, Ma, I practiced swimming all summer!"

Mrs. Rockne shook her head in despair, But she was smiling. "Remember, your father is far away in the United States. You're the man of the family. So you be extra careful!"

"Well, I—I'll try," said Knute.

In the following January a heavy blanket of snow covered the little town of Voss. As Knute went down the street, he kicked happily at deep drifts. He was carrying his skis and a hickory ski pole. When he reached the hardware store, he pushed open the door.

"*Goddag*, Grandpa!" he called to the tall, sturdy man behind the counter. "Is Uncle George here? Can he fix my skis?"

"*Goddag*, Knute! Your uncle is building a sleigh out in the shop. I'll see what I can do."

Grandpa Rockne took one of the skis. It was a flat piece of wood, narrow and long, taller than Knute. "Why, the foot loop is broken." In a few seconds he had repaired it with a piece of wire.

"Thanks a thousand times, Grandpa. The snow is just right for skiing—deep and hard-packed."

"Mind you learn well," his grandfather answered, "if you want to be ski champion of Norway one day."

"I will," Knute said. "I mean, I want to learn to ski well. I don't know whether I'll be a champion!" He and his grandfather both laughed.

Outside, Knute dropped his skis on the snow. He stepped into the foot loops and adjusted his feet firmly. Then he started forward with long sliding steps. With the pole in his right hand, he shoved himself ahead.

Soon he was speeding along the street. He caught sight of another boy just putting on skis. "Thorvald," he called, "want to try some slopes?"

Thorvald Thorvaldson waited for his friend. "Let's go toward the ski jump," he suggested. "There are hills on the way. And maybe we can watch someone jumping."

The two boys set out down the winding street, past the snow-covered frame houses. In a few minutes they were out of the town, in open fields. Ahead, mountains rose higher and higher. They were dotted with fir trees and glistening with snow. The boys climbed slowly around trees and sharp rocks.

At last Knute stopped. "Here's a good place," he said. He could hardly wait to go flying down the hill.

Thorvald looked at the snowy slope. "All right, let's go!"

In two jumps they turned around on the long, awkward skis.

"I'll race you to the road!" Knute shouted.

Both boys shoved hard with their ski poles. They crouched to hold their balance and shot down the slope. They dodged trees and rocks. The wind stung their cheeks and whistled around their ears.

Knute shoved with his pole to get more speed. Slowly he moved ahead of Thorvald. But he came to the road more suddenly than he had expected. He skidded to a quick stop.

Behind him, he heard a crash. He turned, and there was Thorvald, all tangled up in a pine tree! Knute hurried to help him get up. "Are you hurt? What happened?"

Thorvald shook the snow off. "Whew! I'm all right, I guess. There wasn't room to swing around these trees. And—and—I don't **know** how to stop very well!"

"Want me to show you the snow-plow stop? It's easy!"

Thorvald nodded.

"Wait here!" Knute went part way up the slope. "Now watch!" he called. He started down.

He bent his ankles inward so that the inside edges of the skis scraped the snow, instead of sliding smoothly. He brought the points of the skis almost together in front, to form a V. He pressed his ski pole on the snow, dragging it behind him. His skis plowed up the snow, and he came to a quick stop.

"I always get my skis tangled," said Thorvald. "But I'll practice." So he tried to stop several times while Knute watched.

Another skier came streaking down the hill. He stopped suddenly, not a foot away from the boys. It was Olaf Larson. "Well, Knute, have you been off the ski jump today?"

"Off the ski jump?" echoed Knute. What could Olaf mean? None of the younger boys could do that. "Of course not," he answered, "but I will someday!"

"Just the way you swam to that island," Olaf said scornfully.

"Why, I did too swim to that island." Knute was getting angry.

"He's teasing you," said Thorvald.

"You probably can't make even a tiny jump," Olaf taunted. He pointed up the hill. "Could you jump over that ditch?"

"Why—why——" Knute sputtered. He'd learned to ski only that winter, and he hadn't tried any jumping—yet.

Olaf laughed. "Go on, I dare you!"

Knute flushed. "I'll just show you!" He started up the slope.

24

"Don't try it, Knute," begged Thorvald.

But Knute trudged up the slope, above the ditch. Now he turned. "Is this what Ma calls foolish?" he wondered. "But Olaf dared me! I have to show him!"

Knute gave a big shove. Faster and faster he raced down the slope. As he came to the ditch he gave a little spring. Up he went, flying through the air, right over the ditch. It was thrilling!

Knute was so excited he forgot to hold his long skis straight. The ends got crossed. When he hit the snow again, he was thrown off balance. The first thing he knew he was rolling head over heels in a great cloud of snow. His skis flew off. Crash! He had skidded against a rock and bumped his head.

Thorvald and Olaf rushed to him. "Are you all right?" asked Thorvald.

Knute sat up slowly. "Yes," he answered, although he felt dizzy.

"I didn't think you'd really do it," said Olaf. "I was only teasing. It—it was a good jump!"

There was something warm on Knute's face. His hand came away red when he touched it.

"You have a bloody nose!" said Thorvald.

Olaf quickly put some snow on the back of Knute's neck. In a few minutes the nosebleed stopped. Knute got up and put on his skis.

"Now, I'm going to do it again."

"I only dared you once—and you did it."

"Well, I did it wrong. You watch me now!"

Up the slope he went again. When he was ready he thought, "I must keep my skis straight this time." Down he skied. At the ditch, he sailed up and over—and he landed just right!

"Hurrah for Knute!" shouted Thorvald, and Olaf joined in.

"It wasn't a very big jump," said Knute when he joined them. "But I know how to do it now!"

Early in the spring there was a sudden thaw in the town of Voss. On the afternoon of March fourth Knute hurried eagerly toward his home. He was wearing a pair of new shiny rubber boots. He was carrying two trout he had just caught in a near-by stream. He rushed inside the small white house.

"Look, Ma! Can we have these for dinner?"

Mrs. Rockne glanced up from the stove. "Oh, those are nice. But I've cooked a special dinner for your birthday. We'll save your fish until tomorrow."

Knute clumped about the room in his new boots. "See, Martha? See the boots Pa sent me from America?"

He walked heavily across the floor to the big open fireplace in the corner. Little Martha was playing on the hearth rug.

"Better take them off in the house, Knute," said his mother. She smiled. "Though I know you're proud of them!" Knute sat down and pulled off his boots.

Just then Anne came in from school. She flung her books down on a chair. "Oh!" she said, "I have to study for two whole hours this afternoon."

"I wish I could read." Knute was very curious about the books Anne was learning to read.

"Don't worry," she said, "you'll soon have to learn your letters—before you can go to school."

In a short time they all sat down to dinner. "And now, before we eat, I congratulate Knute on his birthday, March fourth!" said Mrs. Rockne, speaking in the Norwegian manner.

"So do I!" said Anne. Knute grinned.

"Finish your soup, Anne," said Mrs. Rockne a few moments later. "Knute is ready for his favorite dish!"

"*Lutfisk?*"

Mrs. Rockne laughed. "I couldn't very well keep it a secret, when I've been soaking it for a week. Now it's cooked just the way you like it."

She gave Knute a big helping of the boiled codfish, with plenty of melted butter on top. She heaped his plate with potatoes.

"I'll bet we have sour-cream porridge, too!" said Knute.

"You've been peeking," said Anne.

Sure enough, they had the thick porridge, with creamy sauce. Then their mother said, "But here's something you don't know about!" She put a plate on the table.

"*Lefse!*" said Knute. On the plate were thin pieces of buttered flat bread, rolled up and covered with sugar. "Everything I like!"

When they had eaten the *lefse* and porridge, it still took a long time to finish the meal. For Mrs. Rockne served another pudding, jellied fruit, bread and butter, cheese and biscuits.

Knute ate and ate. At last he sighed. "I haven't any more room." Then, like all polite Norwegian children, he added, "Thank you for the meal, Ma."

As Anne helped clear away the dishes, Mrs. Rockne said, "Children, I have something to tell you. Your father wants us all to come to the United States—to Chicago!"

"To Chicago!" echoed Knute in surprise.

"Yes, your father likes it so much we're going there to live."

"To live?" echoed Anne. "I like it here!"

Then she and Knute asked question after question. Would they get to ride on a train? Would they sail on a big ship? How long would it take to cross the ocean? How soon would they see Pa? Mrs. Rockne answered them as fast as she could. Finally, Knute started for the door.

"Where are you going?" asked his mother.

"To tie up my skis and skates, so I'll be ready!"

"Oh, we won't leave Voss until May," Mrs. Rockne explained. "Besides, skis are too big to carry across the ocean."

Anne spoke up again. "But, Ma, we won't know anyone in the United States."

"Your father says America is very friendly. Many Norwegians live there. Some of our own relatives live right in Chicago. Lots of people have gone from around here. Why, there are regular Norwegian towns in states named South Dakota, Minnesota, and Wisconsin."

"Leif Ericson really discovered America," Anne put in, "and he was a Norwegian. He sailed there long before Columbus did."

She had already told Knute about the Viking explorer. "All Norwegians are great explorers!" he said proudly.

Mrs. Rockne laughed. "That's not quite true, Knute, but the old Vikings were adventurous. And so are Norwegians today."

"Why do so many go to the United States?"

"It's a land of opportunity," Mrs. Rockne explained. "Here in our small country, with all the mountains, a farmer has a hard time. In the United States, he can have big, level fields of good land for raising crops."

"But Pa isn't a farmer," Anne said.

"No, he wants to work with machines. And America is also the best place for that." Mrs. Rockne sighed. "It *will* be a little strange to us —for a while."

"Where Can
I Ski?"

Knute and Anne were the first passengers off the train when it stopped in the Chicago station. They stood on the platform, looking for Pa. "There he is!" shouted Knute. He ran toward a thin man with long mustaches, who was hurrying to meet them.

Mr. Rockne hugged all the children. He kissed their mother. Everyone talked at once. There was so much to tell Pa about their long trip and their first sight of America. And Pa was amazed to see how much all the children had grown.

Finally he led his family to a carriage to drive

to their new home. Anne and Knute and their mother stared about eagerly. There were so many big buildings! So many people on the sidewalks! So many carriages and wagons on the streets! They drove up a wide avenue, crossed a river and then headed northwest.

After a while they reached a quieter part of town. There were houses instead of shops and office buildings. Trees lined the streets.

"We're coming to Maplewood now," Pa said. "That's the name of the section where we're going to live."

Knute tried to see everything on both sides. "It's so crowded!" he thought. "Where do children play? Where does anyone ski?"

In the next block, on the corner, was a small park. Knute saw a group of boys. One was throwing a ball to another, who tried to hit it with a club. "Look, Pa, what are they doing?"

"They're playing baseball," said Mr. Rockne,

"the national game in the United States. It's as popular here as skiing is in Norway."

Knute turned around to watch as the carriage drove past.

Then he noticed more boys, in a vacant lot between houses. They were kicking a big, odd-shaped ball.

"Is that a game, too?"

"Yes, that's football. It's played mostly in the fall. It's a rough sport."

The games looked strange but exciting. Knute hoped he could learn them soon. Would he throw or kick well enough to play with American boys? He felt a little shy—but eager to try.

"Go to 2521 Rockwell Street," Mr. Rockne told the driver. "Now for my big surprise!"

The carriage stopped before a neat brick house.

"How do you like it, Martha?" asked Mr. Rockne. "I've bought it!"

"Why—why, it's wonderful!" said Mrs. Rockne. "But I thought——"

Knute interrupted. "Are we going to live here?" He jumped from the carriage and started up the walk.

"Knute!" called his father. "Come back, while I explain. The house isn't ready for us yet. In my spare time I'm putting in a new furnace and new floors. Until I finish we'll live in an apartment. You'll have plenty of time to see the house later."

Knute climbed into the carriage again. As they drove on down Rockwell Street, he gazed back at his new home. The brick house looked so foreign, so different from their frame cottage in Voss.

A few blocks away, the carriage drew up before a small apartment house. Mr. Rockne and the driver brought in the baggage. Mrs. Rockne bustled about, unpacking. Anne and Knute, and their father, too, ran here and there as she directed.

At last Mrs. Rockne said, "What about food? How can I go shopping in these American stores?"

"I have some plans," said Mr. Rockne. He smiled broadly. "First, we're all invited to dinner at the Knudtsens' tonight. They're cousins of mine whom you have never seen. Then you children will stay with them while your mother and I go to school."

Anne giggled. "To school!"

"Certainly!" said Mr. Rockne. "I've been going to night classes ever since I came here. Your mother will have to learn English. And we must learn how to be good citizens of this great country!"

"But, Lars," said Mrs. Rockne, "must I go so soon—this first night?"

"There's no use in waiting. In the fall Anne will learn English at her grade school."

"What about me?" Knute asked. "How can I learn English?"

"Well, son, in another year, when you are six, you will go to school."

38

"Everybody else is going to school—except Martha. And she's just a baby. I want to learn English, too."

"You'll pick it up from hearing other people talk," said his mother comfortingly.

Mr. Rockne pulled out his big watch. "Get ready, now," he said. "We don't want to be late in arriving at the Knudtsens' house."

Several weeks later Knute wheeled his new tricycle out to the sidewalk. Pa had brought it home and said, "Knute, I want all you children to have American playthings. See how you like this!" But Knute missed his old toys.

Sometimes, when he missed Thorvald and Olaf, too, he wished he was back in Norway. It was so hot in Chicago! In Norway, now, he would have been up in the cool mountains, swimming in the lake.

Here he couldn't even explore the neighborhood. Ma had said, "Stay right in our block.

There is so much traffic, and the city is strange to us. You mustn't go far away."

Pa had promised to take Knute to the Chicago River or to Lake Michigan to swim. But he had been too busy lately. Today Knute was feeling homesick and lonely and out of sorts.

He sighed. He got on the seat of the tricycle. He pedaled and went bumpety-bump over the rough boards of the sidewalk. He pedaled harder. Faster and faster he went, to the end of the block. "Well, three wheels are better than skis on wooden sidewalks," he thought.

He turned around and started back. He wished he had other boys to play with. He wished he could play one of the ball games. But the children in the neighborhood just stared at him. And Knute didn't know enough English to talk to them.

At the other corner Knute whirled the tricycle around. Then he saw two boys about his own

40

age coming toward him. He had seen them two or three times before. Now they spoke.

"You the new kid in this block?" asked one.

"Where did you get that bike?" asked the other.

Knute wasn't quite sure what they said. He nodded and smiled.

"What's the matter, can't you talk?" asked the first boy. He was chubby and good-natured looking, but he didn't act friendly.

"Aw, he's another dumb Swede," said the dark-haired boy.

"Hey, Ferdy, I'm a Swede—look out who you call dumb!"

Ferdy laughed. "Well, anyway, *he's* dumb. I'll bet he can't even speak English!"

Knute understood that. He got very angry. "Why are they making fun of me?" he thought. Furiously, he pedaled his tricycle right toward the boys.

"Watch out, Otto!" yelled Ferdy.

They sprang aside. Knute rattled down to the corner as fast as he could go. He whirled around and stopped there, glaring at the other boys.

Otto and Ferdy whispered together. Otto took something from his pocket. "Just try that again!" he shouted.

"Why don't you talk?" called Ferdy.

Knute grew even angrier. "I'll show them!" he thought.

He pedaled hard down the sidewalk again, straight at Otto and Ferdy. When he was almost upon them they jumped apart. They were holding a cord between them. Knute tried to stop, but it was too late. *Smack!* The tricycle ran into the cord. Head over heels went Knute, rolling on the sidewalk. He bumped his head and skinned both knees, but he didn't cry. Quickly he stood up.

"Ha, ha, ha!" laughed the boys.

When she heard the noise, Mrs. Rockne looked
out the window. She saw Knute rush at the
boys, his fists flying.

"Take that!" Knute punched Otto in the stomach. Otto sat down, hard. "I'll show them I can
speak English!" Knute said to himself.

"Take that!" he shouted again. He swung at
Ferdy. Ferdy stumbled—and fell down, too.

44

Mrs. Rockne was distressed to see Knute fighting. And she was amazed to hear Knute speak English. She started for the door.

Knute stood, with his fists still up. But he wasn't angry any longer. Otto and Ferdy looked so surprised that Knute began to laugh.

Just then Mrs. Rockne ran out. "Knute, you mustn't fight!"

She looked sternly at Otto and Ferdy. "You boys be friends," she said quietly.

Otto rubbed his stomach. "I don't want to fight him," he said.

"We only teased him because he wouldn't talk," Ferdy said quickly. "My name is Ferdy Wolter. This is Otto Dahl. We'd really like to play with him."

Then Mrs. Rockne remembered. She turned to Knute. "How did you learn to speak English?"

Knute grinned. "I listened."

It's the Best
Game of All

IT WAS A crisp fall day, two years later. Seven-year-old Knute stood waiting at one end of a big vacant lot. "Kick me another, Otto!"

Chunky Otto kicked the football with all his might. As it soared high in the air, Knute got set to catch it. Here it came! He grabbed it tight against his chest and began to run down the field toward the goal.

Otto dashed up, ready to tackle him. Just as Otto drove in low, Knute put on a burst of speed. He stuck out his arm, stiff as a ramrod, and pushed Otto away. The fat boy sprawled full length on the grass. Knute raced across the goal.

"Touchdown!" he shouted as he ran back. "Come on, Otto———"

"No!" Otto sat up slowly. "I've been kicking to you and tackling you until I'm worn out!"

"Maybe you're too fat," Knute teased.

"I'll get you for that." Otto pretended to be angry. He started to get up, then sat down again. "Too much trouble. Why did we have to hurry over here so early?"

"I needed to practice catching punts," said Knute. "I'm not very good at catching."

"Aw, you can catch 'em all right. Anyway, you sure can run." Otto slowly got to his feet.

"Here comes the gang. Hurry up!"

Ferdy ran toward Knute and Otto.

"Hey," he called. "What have you been doing?"

"Oh—just practicing."

"I never saw anyone who loved to practice so much," said Ferdy.

Knute said, "I like everything about football."

"Let's get up a game," one of the boys shouted. "Otto and Ferdy, you choose up sides!"

"All right, I'll take Knute!" Ferdy said.

Otto chose Rudy Rosberg first. In a few seconds they had two teams—but there were only four on a side.

"Six downs to make the field?" Knute asked.

"Sure," said Otto. "We get to receive—Ferdy had first pick."

"Come on, Red, you kick off for us!" shouted Knute.

Red Olson, a big husky boy, called for the ball. He set it on a little mound of dirt at about the middle of the field. Otto and his team spread out to receive.

"Ready?" called Ferdy.

"Ready!" Otto answered.

Red ran forward and kicked. But he topped the ball. It bounced crazily down the field. All the boys chased after it. Edgar Eke, the biggest boy on Otto's side, reached it first. He grabbed it up and started to run.

Knute went toward him as fast as he could run. Otto tried to knock him out of the way, but Knute dodged. Edgar, running hard, tried to straight-arm Knute. Knute ducked under his arm and tackled him hard around the thighs.

"Wow! What a tackle!" shouted Ferdy.

Knute jumped up, smiling. He was tingling with excitement.

Now Edgar got ready to center the ball for his side. Otto lined up beside him. Rudy was quarterback, and Dick Abrams, their other player, was halfback.

"Knute, you and Red and Al play in the line," said Ferdy. "I'll stay back."

Knute got ready to charge in again and tackle the ball carrier. Edgar snapped the ball back to Rudy. Knute started after Rudy. But he wasn't watching Otto! Otto plowed into him, and they went down in a heap.

"Got you that time!" said Otto.

The next time Rudy tossed the ball to Dick. Again Otto blocked Knute out of the play. Dick ran past for a good gain before Ferdy finally brought him down.

Knute was angry with himself. He shouldn't let Otto block him out. On the next play he dodged Otto and caught Rudy before he could get started.

Up and down the field the teams moved. Knute ran and tackled and blocked. He was having the time of his life.

Finally Otto said, "Hey, we'd better stop. I'm hungry. It must be suppertime."

"We win, 36-32!" shouted Ferdy.

"Aw, that's only because we have to stop," said Edgar. "We'll play you again tomorrow."

"Won't someone practice blocking with me?"

asked Knute. "Come on, Ferdy!" He darted toward Ferdy, but his friend was quick. He leaped aside and gave Knute a hard push. Knute skidded on the ground. All the boys laughed.

Knute jumped up. "See, I need practice!"

The boys laughed louder.

"I have to go home," said Ferdy, "and so do you, Knute Rockne!"

"Don't you ever have enough?" asked Otto.

"No! Ferdy, I'll race you home!"

Anne's birthday came on Sunday. That day it turned very cold. There had been a snowfall during the night. But the Rocknes all liked cold weather. They were glad to go out to church.

After dinner Knute gave Anne her present. "Congratulations on your birthday, Anne!"

"Thank you, Knute." She unwrapped the package quickly. "A book!"

She opened it and leafed through it. Suddenly she raised her head and stared at Knute.

"Why," she said, "this is the book about Columbus *you* were so crazy to read! You bought it just so you could read it!"

Knute's face got red. His parents laughed.

"All right, Mr. Knute Rockne. But you don't get to see this book until I've finished it all!"

"Oh, Anne," said her mother, still laughing, "don't be cross! It's really a very nice present."

"But it's *my* birthday!" Anne said.

"Please don't be cross," said Knute. "If you let me read it when you're through—then you can buy me a doll for my birthday!"

Mr. and Mrs. Rockne laughed again—and this time Anne joined in.

"Now all of you get your hats and coats," said Mr. Rockne. "I'm going to take you skating at Lincoln Park!"

"Hurrah!" shouted Knute. He ran to find everyone's skates. Even little Martha had a tiny pair Mr. Rockne had made for her.

Winter weather meant football was over for the year, but skating was a fine sport, too!

A year later eleven boys were lined up in formation on a muddy football field.

"Signals!" called Rudy. "16-44-35! 53-21-76! 45-12-22!"

Edgar, playing center, snapped the ball back to Rudy. He pitched it to Dick at halfback.

Knute was at right end. He and the rest of the team charged forward at an imaginary team. Dick cut through the line with the ball, then stopped and tossed it to Edgar. The "Tricky Tigers" were holding signal drill.

"Call my number, Rudy!" begged Knute, running up and down excitedly. "Let's try the end-around play!"

"Give me time! We must call 'em all!"

"Let's go, gang!" called Knute.

The team lined up again. "Signals!" Rudy barked. "42-36-17! 37-18-95!"

Knute got ready. Forty-two was his signal to carry the ball.

"14-17-86! 35-45-65! 19-27-64!" Rudy went on and on. But he didn't call the number to start the play.

Knute kept expecting it every second. He made a false start, but quickly jumped back into position. All the boys laughed at him.

But Knute felt cross. "You've ruined the play! And we have a game this afternoon!"

Then he understood that Rudy had played a joke on him. He began to laugh, too.

"You were so anxious!" said Rudy. "I wanted to see if I could make you start too soon. And I did!"

Ferdy exclaimed, "Here come the Avondales!"

Rudy whistled. "Boy, they're big!"

Knute watched the Avondale boys walking down the street and onto the field. They *were* big! He looked over the Tricky Tigers. Edgar,

54

at center, and Otto, at guard, and Red, at full-back, were the only ones as big as the smallest Avondale!

"The bigger they come, the harder they fall!" he said. He was trying to sound cheerful. But in his heart he was afraid the Tigers would lose.

"Start the game!" shouted one Avondale player.

Edgar flipped a coin with Mac McCoy, the Avondale captain. Mac won, and chose to receive. The Avondales spread out over their end of the field.

In a second Red would kick off. The Tigers formed their line across the field.

"Ready?" called Edgar.

"Ready!" Mac yelled.

Knute was tingling all over. His heart seemed to be in his mouth. He was eager to begin—but he couldn't help feeling nervous in that moment waiting for the kickoff.

Red ran forward. He kicked the ball solidly. *Plunk!* It soared end over end down the field. The game was on!

Knute shot forward, pell-mell with the rest of the Tigers. The minute he could move he felt better.

The ball bounced and rolled toward the big Avondale captain. Mac scooped up the ball and headed across the field away from Knute. He dodged Ferdy, but just then Knute threw himself headlong at Mac, catching him around the waist. Now Knute knew what it was to run into a brick wall! But he hung on; down they went.

Knute was dizzy when he got up. But he was feeling good, just the same. He always did when he'd made a hard tackle.

"Let's stop 'em, Tigers!" yelled Otto. The two teams lined up, getting set for the next play. The Avondale center passed the ball. The Avondale boys in the middle of the line charged forward.

Edgar and Otto were swept aside as Mac plowed right through center for a long gain. Red finally tackled him.

Knute was worried as he ran back to his position. These Avondales were so big! "Dig in and stop 'em, Otto!" he called.

The ball was snapped. Knute charged ahead. The play was coming his way!

A tall Avondale boy tried to block Knute. Knute side-stepped and started after the ball carrier. He was about to tackle him when the Avondale blocker grabbed his leg and pulled him down. The runner swept past, but at last Dick tackled him.

Knute jumped up. "Cut out that holding!"

"Aw, you tripped yourself!"

Red rushed over. "If we had a referee, that'd cost you fifteen yards!"

The Avondale captain said, "No holding, now, Jack. Come on, let's go!"

58

They lined up again. It was the same play! Jack rushed at Knute to block him. Again Knute dodged. And again Jack grabbed his foot.

Knute wanted to fight! He doubled up his fists to go at Jack—no matter how big he was. But then he stopped. Jack was breaking the rules by holding—but there was a worse penalty for fighting. "There must be some way to make him stop," Knute mumbled to himself, "some way besides fighting!"

On the next play the Avondales fumbled. Al Jessupp, at left guard, pounced on the ball for the Tigers.

"Our ball!" shouted Otto.

Knute dashed up to Rudy. "Run one right at Jack," he urged.

Rudy nodded.

Knute hurried back to Red's brother Bill, who played right tackle alongside him. He whispered in Bill's ear.

"Signals!" Rudy called.

The teams lined up. Knute eyed Jack, across the line from him. Back went the ball. Bill and Knute charged at Jack. Knute drove at Jack's legs. Bill charged high into the boy.

"Oof!" gasped Jack as the two Tigers brought him down.

60

Red came charging through the hole. He cut out toward the side line and raced to a touchdown.

Bill and Knute jumped up. Jack slowly got to his feet.

"That's the way *we* block," Bill said. "Fair and square!"

Jack muttered and turned away. But he didn't try holding Knute any more that afternoon.

As the game wore on, the Tigers found they couldn't stop the powerful Avondale rushes. The Tigers were covered with mud and bruises before the game was over. Knute charged and tackled a man with all his strength—but the game ended 18-12 in favor of the Avondales.

Ferdy walked home with Knute. "All these teams around Logan Square are too big for us," he complained.

"We could stop 'em if we'd practice blocking and tackling more!"

Ferdy laughed. "Maybe you're right, Knute. Anyway, I'm glad the ground was soft today."

Knute wiped some of the mud off his face.

"Say, you've got a black eye!"

Knute touched his eye. "It *is* a little sore." He smeared the mud back on his face. "Can you see it now?"

"No. Your face is as muddy as your clothes."

At the Rockne house Knute suggested, "Come on in and have an apple and a glass of milk."

The boys walked in quietly. Mrs. Rockne was busy arranging blankets in a cradle. She was rocking the new baby. "Well, Knute," she said without looking up, "what have you and Ferdinand been doing?"

"Why, playing football."

"Football?" Mrs. Rockne glanced at the boys. "Knute, what's happened to you and Ferdy?"

"Why—why, nothing, Ma. It was just a little muddy, that's all."

"Ferdinand Wolter, you'd better go straight home. I want to talk to Knute."

Ferdy looked scared at her tone. He nodded, without a word, and hurried out.

"Knute, you shouldn't be playing that rough game. Why—why, you could be killed! It—it's just fighting!"

"Oh, no, Ma, really it isn't! It's a wonderful game. All the boys around here play."

"Don't try to talk your way out! I won't allow you to play football!"

Knute's heart sank. What could he do? He wanted to tell Ma about the game, and why he loved it. But he realized she wouldn't understand. "All right," he said slowly, "but——"

"But what?"

"Well, Pa says he wants me to play all the American games."

Mrs. Rockne smiled. She was relieved that Knute wasn't hurt—dirty as he was. "I'll speak to your father," she said. "Now you run along and clean up."

Knute hoped that Pa would convince Ma that football was all right.

But after supper Pa said, "Knute, I have to agree with your mother: football is too rough."

Knute looked very sad. "Pa, it's the best game of all! And you always said I should learn American sports!"

"You don't need much urging! But you can play baseball. Your mother and I both think that's a nice, safe game. Yes, sir, that's all right."

"Somebody'll get my place on the team. The boys will all say I'm a sissy."

"I hardly think so, Knute."

"But, Pa, I practice a lot! You always say, 'Learn to do a thing perfectly, and you'll be all right.' Isn't that so?"

Mr. Rockne cleared his throat. "Knute, I like persistence, but this time the answer must be no.

Besides, you're still small for your age, you know. We don't want you to get hurt."

"But I'm strong, Pa. I can run all day!"

Mr. Rockne shook his head. "I'm sorry, Knute. Your mother has a lot to do for the new baby and for the girls. I don't want her worried about what you're doing. So let's say no more about it. There will be no more football."

Knute hadn't thought about that. "All right, Pa." He had to do what Pa and Ma said. But he wanted so much to play! "Well," he thought, "the season's almost over, anyway. Maybe by next year—" But Pa had been so firm that Knute was afraid he would say no even then.

Knute sighed. He wondered what he could do while the fellows were playing football. Then he had an idea. "I'll get a job! Maybe I can run errands for the drugstore. Then I can save up for a baseball. I'll make money, and then I can buy anything I want, without asking Pa! I'll buy my own books and presents for the girls." That made him remember the Columbus book.

He got it from the bookcase. He settled down to read it for the fourth time. He was soon deep in the story. But somehow it didn't seem quite so good this time. For Knute couldn't entirely forget football!

Knute Is
Stubborn

IT WAS THE following spring. One Saturday Knute and Ferdy were walking to the vacant lot. "How do you like this?" asked Knute.

"What?"

Knute tossed Ferdy a new baseball.

"Official National League Ball!" Ferdy read. "Where'd you get it?"

"I saved up my errand money—what I earned while the rest of you were playing football."

As they reached the field Ferdy said, "Come on, I'll knock out some flies."

Knute punched his glove with his fist and got ready. Ferdy sent a low liner to his right. Like lightning Knute raced for the ball. He managed to catch it just before it hit the ground.

It felt good to be playing ball again. He was glad Ma and Pa approved of baseball!

Soon the other boys arrived.

"Hey, we've got a game this afternoon," Otto announced. "I told Harry Jackson to bring the Maplewoods over."

"Here they come!" said Knute.

"Can we use your new ball?" asked Ferdy.

"Sure," said Knute.

The Maplewood boys threw Knute's ball back and forth for a while to get warmed up. Then the game got underway.

Knute and Ferdy and Al trotted to the outfield. Knute pounded his glove. "Strike 'em out!" he shouted to Rudy, who was pitching.

For three innings neither side was able to score. Then in the last of the fourth, Knute went up to bat. He was determined to get on base.

He stood in the batter's box waggling his bat.
The Maplewood pitcher threw one straight for
the plate. Knute swung with all his might. But
he hit the ball on top, and it just dribbled along
the ground toward the third baseman. Knute
tore down the first-base line, and made it safely.

Al came up and struck out, but Knute stole second. Otto hit a grounder to the first base-man. He was an easy out, but Knute ran to third base.

Then Ferdy came to bat. He took two hard swings, but fouled the ball each time. The pitcher wound up. Knute got set to race for home with the first run, if Ferdy could only get on base. The pitcher threw the ball. Ferdy started to swing. Something seemed to stop his bat, and he swung through very slowly. He missed the ball.

"That's the third out!" crowed the Maplewood catcher. He took off his mask.

Ferdy shouted, "You topped my bat! I'm not out!"

All the Maplewood players threw down their gloves and ran in to take their turn at bat. But the Tigers jumped up and surrounded the Maple-wood catcher.

70

"That's interference!"

"It's illegal! Ferdy goes to first!"

"Aw, he struck out!" growled the Maplewood catcher.

Both teams crowded around Ferdy and the catcher. Everyone was arguing at the top of his voice. Somebody shoved Otto, and he took a swing at a Maplewood player. Several boys picked up bats and waved them threateningly.

Knute ran in from third. Just as he reached the crowd, Harry swung back with his bat. He didn't see Knute, and his bat caught Knute squarely in the face.

The blow knocked him down and for a minute everything went black to Knute. When his head cleared, his eyes were watering so much that he couldn't see. He covered his face with his hands. "Oh," he groaned, "does that hurt!"

The other boys had stopped quarreling. Ferdy leaned down and pulled Knute's hands away.

"Let's see your face," he said. "Where did it hit you?"

Knute's nose was bleeding and his face had already begun to swell. He tried to laugh. "Ha, ha, ha! I think that bat broke my nose!"

Otto was alarmed. "Gee! Knute must be out of his head!"

"We'd better take him home." Ferdy helped Knute up. Harry brought him a wet handkerchief to hold over his nose.

"Don't you see?" Knute said. "Ma and Pa say football is too rough—and then I break my nose playing baseball."

Now Otto understood.

Ferdy said, "It *is* sort of funny, but I don't see how *you* can laugh. Come on, I'll walk home with you."

In a few minutes Knute felt better, although his head throbbed and every bone in his face hurt.

"Oh, oh," said Ferdy, "you've got two black eyes!"

"I hope they get good and black."

"Will your mother and father let you play football now?"

"Sure," said Knute. "How could I get hurt any worse at that?"

Ferdy shook his head doubtfully. "I hope you're right. We need you back at end. But I don't know if your parents will agree."

But Knute was sure. And he was determined. He *had* to play football again!

At home Knute didn't say anything about football right away. Ma had been so surprised and worried about his broken nose. She couldn't understand how it could have happened. Baseball seemed such a nice game!

But Knute had a plan. He had seen a wonderful pair of padded football pants in a shop window in Logan Square. If he could only get those thick pants, and some shin guards, maybe Ma and Pa would let him play. Maybe Ma could sew some pads on an old sweater. Maybe, if he worked hard, he could even buy a headgear.

So Knute kept on running errands for the Maplewood Pharmacy. And he got a newspaper route, so he could earn a little more.

One spring afternoon when he came home from school, Knute saw a man tacking a sign on the Rockne house. What could this be? Knute broke into a run.

The sign read SCARLET FEVER.

Knute rushed inside. "Ma, who's got scarlet fever?"

"No one yet," said Mrs. Rockne, "and I pray that no one will!"

"Then why is that sign on the house?"

"Martha's been exposed," Mrs. Rockne explained. "Now all you children will have to stay inside for six weeks."

Knute was horrified. He wouldn't be able to deliver papers or work for the drugstore to earn money—he wouldn't be able to play baseball—and he'd get far behind in school.

"Ma, I can't! That'll ruin my plans. And when nobody is sick, it's silly!"

"I'm afraid you'll have to, Knute," Mrs. Rockne said. "That's the quarantine law."

Six weeks—forty-two days. They dragged by. Knute was very restless, especially when he watched the other boys pass his house on their way to the field. But he didn't get scarlet fever. Neither did his sisters.

One afternoon he said, "Couldn't I just run over to the field and watch the fellows play?"

Mrs. Rockne smiled. "No, Knute, I can't let you go out."

"But I'll get weak. I won't be able to do anything if I just sit around."

His mother laughed. "You're a pretty strong

75

boy. You are small for your age, and that's one reason I worried about your playing football. But staying in six weeks isn't going to hurt you."

Knute decided this would be a good time to tell Ma about his plan.

"And I'll buy the pants as soon as I can earn the money," he ended. "Then if you'll fix my sweater with pads, I can't get hurt."

"Well, I don't know——"

"Ma, it was just an accident when I hurt my nose. It wouldn't happen again! Besides football isn't any more dangerous than baseball."

"Well, I'll talk to your father," Mrs. Rockne promised.

"I've just got to play!" Knute declared.

That night Knute lay awake for a long time, wondering what Ma and Pa would decide.

In their room Mrs. Rockne was saying, "Knute wants to play football again. But since he broke his nose, I'm afraid of *all* the games!"

"Perhaps Knute knows more about them than we do. We thought baseball would be safe, but look what happened. Maybe we should let him play football."

"Oh, Lars!"

"Well, the boy must learn to stand on his own two feet. Yes, I think we'd better let him play."

Mrs. Rockne sighed. "Perhaps you're right. But some of the boys he plays with are so big and rough."

Mr. Rockne chuckled. "Knute may be small, but he's strong. He can stand up to those bigger boys."

Knute was overjoyed when he heard the news. "I'll be careful," he promised. Now he'd have to get busy.

Finally the six-week quarantine was ended. Knute burst out of the house the first morning and raced off down the block.

"Where are you going?" shouted Ferdy.

Knute halted at the corner to wait for his friend. "To school, of course. I'll race you!" He was in high spirits, just to be out of doors again.

"Don't be in such a hurry. Miss Cooper's giving us a test today."

"I hope I haven't missed too much."

"My gosh, you sound as though you *liked* school!"

"Sure," said Knute. "Besides, Pa says what's the use of going to school if you don't learn all you can?"

"Maybe so, but you don't have to like it! Is there anything you *don't* like?"

"Staying home for six weeks."

"We missed you at the field."

"Ferdy, I can play football this fall!"

"How'd you ever talk your Mother into it?"

Knute told him all about his plan. "Say, that's a good idea!" Ferdy said. "We all ought to save up and buy real uniforms."

They met Otto at the door of the Brentano School. All the way to their room they talked about outfitting the football team that fall.

In the classroom Miss Cooper rapped for order. "Change seats for the test."

Everyone got up and moved across the aisle to another seat. The teacher wrote the questions on the blackboard.

A lot of the questions bothered Knute. It seemed as though he couldn't get the right answers. He chewed his pencil. He wrote slowly. Finally time was up. The children exchanged papers for grading. When Knute got his back, it was marked 82. Knute was upset. He had never before had a grade lower than 90.

At noon Miss Cooper said, "Knute, you did very well to get an 82, considering how long you've been out."

"But I can't understand it. I should have known all those answers!"

Miss Cooper smiled. "You'll do better next time," she assured him. "Don't worry about it."

But Knute did worry. He was determined it wouldn't happen again. Every evening after baseball and his errands and his paper route he did his homework with special care. He worked over and over every exercise he had to hand in.

A short time later, Miss Cooper gave another test. "Change seats," she said to the class. Everyone in the room got up to move except Knute.

Otto said to him, "Get up—I have to sit there."

Miss Cooper looked around from the blackboard. "What's the trouble?"

"Miss Cooper, I—I don't want to move."

"Why, Knute, that's the rule. You never take a test in your own seat."

Knute looked unhappy, but determined. "Miss Cooper, I got a low grade the last time I moved. It's bad luck. I—I want to sit here."

The teacher explained that Knute's long absence had caused his grade. But he didn't believe it. He didn't like to have all the children looking at him, laughing, but he was determined not to change seats.

"All right," said Miss Cooper, "we'll go ahead. Everyone except Knute. When you're ready to move, Knute, you may take the test."

Knute thought, "Now what am I going to do? All I want is to get a good mark." But he was stubborn. He wouldn't move!

Noontime came, and all the pupils went home for lunch—except Knute. Miss Cooper sent Ferdy to the next grade for Anne.

She told her brother, "Go ahead and change your seat! Don't be so silly!"

Still he wouldn't move. Anne brought him a sandwich from home for lunch. The afternoon wore on. At the end of the day, Knute began to think about playing baseball. And carrying papers. What should he do?

82

The bell rang. All the other children filed out. The teacher came back to Knute's desk. "I'll just have to mark you zero for this test."

He couldn't have a zero on his record! "I'll move," Knute said finally. He got up and went across the aisle to Otto's seat. Miss Cooper gave him a new set of questions. When he had finished, she graded his paper. And he got 98! Knute breathed a sigh of relief.

"Knute, what got into you? There is nothing unlucky about changing seats. You always work hard—that's what makes good luck!"

Knute grinned sheepishly. "I guess it was silly, but I was sure it was the seat that brought me bad luck. I—I know better now."

Knute hurried out. He was already late for baseball!

"Who Carries the Ball?"

"HEY, FERDY," called Knute, as school let out one day near the end of the term, "come on over to Humboldt Park with me."

"Aren't you going to play baseball today?"

"Sure, but I saw a notice in the newspaper this morning about a track meet for boys! Let's find out what's happening."

Otto said he wanted to come with them. So the three boys hurried several blocks south to the public park. The boys edged in, eager to see everything.

There were boys in track suits of all kinds, and even some boys in regular clothes. They were running and jumping and vaulting, warming up for the track meet.

"Why," said Knute, "some of those runners are no bigger than we are. There are races for all different ages, the paper said. With medals and everything. I wish we could get in."

"Why couldn't we?" said Otto. "Let's go ask."

"You can't," said Ferdy. "You have to belong to a club or the YMCA or something and be entered ahead of time."

Knute watched the runners with mounting excitement. "I know," he said. "Why don't we get up our own track team?"

"You bet!" said Ferdy. "Let's get the gang over here tomorrow and practice. Anyone can use the park."

The next day all the Tigers showed up at the park. They were talking and arguing loudly about the different races. Each Tiger was sure he could win the fifty-yard dash. Except Otto.

"The rest of you can run," he said. "I'll save myself for the shot-put."

There was a chorus of howls about Otto's laziness. Otto just laughed. "I'll be the official starter," he said. He pulled out a watch. "We've got to run this like a regular meet. Come on now, line up for the fifty-yard dash!"

All the other Tigers lined up across the track, ready to run.

"On your mark—get set—*go!*" Otto shouted.

The boys charged forward. In his eagerness to get away quickly, Knute's foot slipped, and he dropped a step or two behind. But he almost caught up. Rudy finished first, Ferdy second and Knute third—by inches.

But in the hundred-yard dash Knute made a good start. He pounded down the track, ahead all the way. He streaked across the finish line first and pulled up, puffing. "What's the next race?" he gasped.

"No race," said Otto. "Now we'll have the shot-put."

The boys didn't have a regular twelve-pound iron ball. They decided to use a big rock they found. Otto and Edgar were best at this. They hurled the rock farther than any of the others.

They tried high-jumping and broad-jumping. Then they tried hurdle racing. But nobody could get over all the hurdles! The boys banged their shins and skinned their knees, as they knocked down the hurdles and sprawled on the track. Even so, they all wanted to try pole vaulting— but they didn't have any pole.

"Well, then, out for the half-mile run!" Otto announced.

"Whew!" sighed Ferdy. "Half a mile after all this?"

Knute trotted up to the starting line. He might be small, but he'd show everybody he could run.

No one else was very eager to try the half mile.

Finally Al and Bill decided to race. Off they went! The first time around the track, the three boys were close together. But the second time around, Knute speeded up. Gradually he pulled farther and farther ahead. Al and Bill puffed and strained, but they couldn't overtake Knute.

"How did you do it?" said Ferdy afterward.

Knute was panting. "I—I guess," he puffed, "it's just—just because I like to run."

"Now for the mile run!" Otto bawled.

"Wait a minute," Knute said. "I want to run that, too."

"You're crazy," said Ferdy. "That's too much!"

Knute just grinned.

"Come on, Red," said Edgar. "Somebody's got to run against him."

So Edgar and Red, the two biggest boys, lined up with Knute. Knute looked so small beside them the boys all laughed. "You can't win this time," Otto warned.

The first time around, Red was ahead, with Edgar second and Knute close behind. The second time around, Knute pulled ahead. The third time around, Edgar was winded. He had to stop. Knute and Red were the only ones left.

As he came near the finish line, Knute put on a burst of speed. He dashed across and threw himself on the ground to catch his breath.

Red came puffing across the line and flung himself down beside Knute. "It's too much for me! I'm worn out."

Knute sat there breathing hard, his face red and perspiring. But he felt happy. The bigger boys might shove him around in games—but he could show them when it came to running. Besides, it was good practice for football.

It was a busy summer for Knute and the Tigers. They played baseball. They practiced running and jumping. They went swimming in the Chicago River and in Lake Michigan.

Knute kept up his paper route and ran errands for the Maplewood Pharmacy. He did all the other odd jobs he could find. Slowly his pile of nickels and dimes grew larger.

One afternoon late in the summer Knute walked into the house, whistling. He carried a big package under his arm.

In the front room, Pa was listening to Martha practice her piano lesson. "Well, I guess that's enough for today," he was saying. He looked up. "Hello, son. What tune is that?"

"Why, that's 'Go, Chicago'! It's the university's football song."

"I hope someday to send you to the University of Chicago. Let's see if I can play that tune."

Mr. Rockne opened his violin case and quickly tuned his violin. Then he struck up the tune. Knute sang the words, and Martha hummed.

"Pa," said Knute when they had finished, "wouldn't that sound better on the trumpet?"

"All right, the trumpet then." Mr. Rockne took out his shiny trumpet.

Anne came in. "I don't want to miss anything," she said. So they all joined in. The Rocknes loved to sing and play together. They took turns suggesting songs.

"Knute," said his father, "you've got a pretty good voice. Yes, indeed. Maybe you'll be a musician. Perhaps I ought to get you a flute."

"Oh, no!" Anne covered her ears.

Knute laughed. "Or some drums," he said with a mischievous glance at Anne.

"Oh," Anne groaned, "that'd be worse."

Mrs. Rockne looked in. "If you're all through, the girls had better come help me in the kitchen."

When they were alone Knute picked up his package. "Pa, I want to show you something."

He tore off the wrappings. He pulled out a pair of football pants. "What do you think of 'em?" His eyes were shining.

92

"Well, I'm no expert on football pants. But they look well padded, son. They should save you many a bruise."

"I—I want to play this fall, Pa."

"All right, I promised! I must say I admire your persistence," he added, with a smile.

At the vacant lot a few weeks later Knute was the only Tiger with a new pair of pants. All the boys admired them.

"We'd better earn money and buy some, too," said Ferdy.

"See what I have!" Otto put on a big black rubber nose guard. It fastened with a strap around his head, and at the bottom he held it in his mouth. It looked like a false face. All the boys howled with laughter.

"Well, I didn't get it to look pretty," said Otto. "It's rough there in the center of the line!"

"We'd better practice," Rudy said.

The boys got into formation. Rudy barked

signals. They ran through play after play. Knute, at his right-end position, charged eagerly on each one. Up and down he ran tirelessly. But at the same time he was thinking hard, too.

Most of the plays went right through center. Rudy would give the ball to big Red. Red would charge straight ahead, while Edgar and Otto and Al made interference for him. But so many of the teams the Tigers played had tall, chunky boys in the line. It was hard to make yardage through them. "We ought to surprise them, somehow," thought Knute. "Do something they don't expect."

"Hey, Rudy," he called, "don't we have too many line plunges?"

"What's wrong with them?" asked Red. "It's the surest way to pile up the yards."

"But everybody does that," said Knute. "Some of those big teams can stop us every time. We ought to surprise them!"

94

"Oh," said Red, "you mean with more plays where the end carries the ball?"

Everybody laughed. Knute's face got red. But he kept on explaining his idea. "We have fast runners on our team," he argued. "If the other side is expecting a line plunge, we could run a trick play and get around those big boys. Then we could outrun them."

"Aw, he just wants to carry the ball," Red said.

"Look at these crisscross plays." Knute took a stick and made marks in the dirt to show how they went. The boys were all interested as Knute explained. "Red gets the ball and starts off to the left, and the other team goes after him. But then he hands the ball to Dick, and Dick runs back around to the right before they know what's happened!"

The boys talked it over and agreed to try it out.

"Aw, it's too tricky!" said Red.

"No, it isn't," the others shouted. "It's good! Come on, let's try it."

So they kept working until they had it right.

"Now I have one more idea," said Knute. "A triple pass in the backfield."

"Wow!" said Ferdy.

"That's too much," Red said.

"Not if we work it right," Knute insisted. He showed them how to make the play. Back and forth the ball went, and back again.

"But who carries it?" Red asked.

"Why," said Knute, "the—the right end!"

"I knew it!" Red said. "Knute made up this play for himself."

The boys were chuckling, but Ferdy spoke up. "Well, he's a fast runner. If he can get loose on that play, it's a sure touchdown."

The boys tried it out. It was a hard play to master. But Knute insisted they keep on trying until it was right.

"I'm dizzy!" Red said finally. "I don't know where the ball is, myself."

"We'll make the other side dizzy, too," said Knute.

So the boys chose sides and battled up and

down the field. Knute was happy to be playing again. He was glad the team liked his ideas. He was sure they would work.

They did work, too. The Tigers won most of their games that season. And they surprised their old rivals, the Avondales, with the triple backfield pass!

"Go, You Tigers!"

ONE SUNDAY afternoon two years later Mr. Rockne asked Knute to help him build some shelves. Knute and his father carried several long pieces of lumber down to the basement. Mr. Rockne had a workbench there.

"Now we'll put the shelves here in the corner," he explained. He opened his folding rule and started to measure the wall.

Knute pulled two sawhorses out of the corner and laid the lumber across them. "All ready, Pa."

"All right, Knute. Mark off four pieces 36 inches long." While his father ruled off the wall,

Knute measured the lumber with a yardstick. He thought it would be easy. But the wood was coarse-grained and his pencil slipped. He measured and drew the marks over again. The lines still looked rather wavy, but it seemed that he couldn't get them more accurate.

"I'll look at those before we start sawing," said Mr. Rockne. He measured them quickly.

"Why, these two are wrong! You should be more careful." Swiftly he corrected the mark. Knute watched him closely, trying to see what he had done wrong.

"You saw off one board while I nail up some strips," said Mr. Rockne.

"I'll do this right!" Knute thought. Carefully he set the saw blade on the mark. Slowly, he pulled up. The saw bounced off the mark and cut deep into the edge of the piece of lumber. It also nicked his finger. "I'll get this yet," Knute muttered. He began again. He sawed along the line steadily. Suddenly he noticed how crooked it looked. He had got away from the line! He tried to saw back toward the line. The saw squeaked loudly.

Mr. Rockne stepped over to see what was the matter. He took one look at the crooked sawing and the scarred wood. *"Klureneve!"* he said sharply. Pa was really angry when he started talking Norwegian! "You're all thumbs!"

"I'll do it right," said Knute stubbornly. "I'll try it again."

Mr. Rockne sighed. "Knute, I guess you just don't have a knack with tools."

"You fix this one, and let me try another."

"No, sir. I haven't enough lumber for that. I know you'd work at it all day—but that's too expensive!"

Mr. Rockne picked up the saw. With a few deft strokes he finished the piece Knute had started. He turned to Knute, with a twinkle in

his eye. "You know, son, it seems odd that you're not clumsy down at the drugstore. Maybe it's because you get paid there!"

Knute was embarrassed. "I—I——"

"I was only teasing you. I'm glad you can earn extra money. I'm just disappointed that you don't like tools as I do. I like to work with tools, as you like sports."

"Say, Pa, we have a big football game on Saturday and ——"

"Just a minute. I'm glad you're playing these games. They're good for you. But I don't want you to forget everything else."

"What do you mean, Pa?"

"You're a bright boy, Knute. And I want to give you a fine education. I'll send you to college, if you show me you're serious about getting ahead."

Knute was puzzled. "I always get good grades in school——"

"That's right. And keep it up. You mustn't let your sports interfere."

"Why, they don't, Pa."

"I just want to caution you. You see, I hope to send all the girls through school," Pa went on. "That will take a lot of money. So I must be sure you're serious about schoolwork, before I send you to college."

"Sure, Pa." Knute had never thought much about college. It seemed very far away. He was only eleven—not even in high school yet. "Pa?"

"Yes?"

"Don't you want me to help with the shelves?"

Mr. Rockne laughed. "I got to talking so much I almost forgot them. No, you'd better run along. You'd saw up yourself instead of that lumber in no time at all!"

"Where's Otto?" all the Tigers were asking. It was Saturday noon. They were waiting at the field, carrying their football clothes. A few of

104

the boys had headgears now. Most of them had padded pants. A few of the linemen had shin guards. There were even a few pairs of football shoes. But no two sweaters were alike.

"He told me he'd have a surprise," said Knute. "No telling what it may be."

"But we have to get over to the White Sox ball park in time for the game," Rudy said excitedly.

"Look," said Ferdy. "Why—Otto!"

Around the corner came a wagon, driven by Otto, and pulled by—a big long-eared mule! The boys all stared in astonishment. Then they rushed over to the wagon with howls of laughter.

"Here's our carriage," said Otto. "Jump in!"

The boys piled in at once. Otto slapped the mule with the reins. Away they went, jogging slowly through the Chicago streets.

"Say, this is Mr. Geddes' delivery wagon!"

"Sure!" said Otto. "And what's more, I can borrow it any Saturday we play far away."

"Hurrah!" shouted Ferdy. "Now we can take on anybody in Chicago!"

"We'd better beat the Hamburg Athletic Club today," said Rudy. "They'll be tough."

"Aw, we'll beat 'em," said Red. "Then we'll be the twelve-year-old champions of Chicago."

"How do you figure that?"

"Well, nobody's beaten Hamburg yet, and nobody's beaten us. It's simple!"

The boys talked and laughed as they jolted along in the wagon. Then Knute started singing "Go, You Tigers!" to the tune of "Go, Chicago!" The others joined in. They were singing loudly when they reached the park.

"Look at the crowd!" said Knute in surprise. People were standing all around the field.

In the dressing room the Tigers got into their football clothes.

"We'll have a real referee," said Red. "Hamburg plays in a regular league."

106

The Tigers were sprinting up and down when the Hamburg team pushed through the crowd. They were all wearing complete equipment. They had orange jerseys and new canvas jackets.

"They look like a *real* team," Rudy said.

"Well, they can't beat us with uniforms," said Knute. But he was alarmed at their size.

"Better run some plays," Rudy called.

The Tigers jumped into formation. In spite of Knute's hopeful words, they were a little nervous. They weren't used to a crowd. The Hamburg boys were pretty big, and the uniforms did look impressive.

Edgar ran over and flipped a coin with the Hamburg captain. "We receive," he said.

"Let's go, fellows!" Knute shouted.

The Tigers spread out over their end of the field to receive the kickoff. Knute danced up and down. "Hit 'em hard," he shouted. He was tingling with excitement.

"Ready?" called the referee. Both sides called, "Ready!"

The Hamburg kicker started toward the ball, and the rest of the team followed him.

Knute thought his heart would stop. Then the ball came soaring through the air, and Knute was off like a shot. He darted across the field to make interference for Dick, who scooped up the ball.

Down the field Knute charged. He lunged at the first orange sweater. They went down in a heap. "Well, Hamburg falls like anybody else," thought Knute. He struggled to jump up, to block someone else, but Dick was already down.

"Signals!" Rudy called.

The two teams lined up. Face to face, the Hamburg boys looked bigger than ever.

Edgar snapped the ball. The teams charged. Rudy gave the ball to Red, who tried to plow through the center of the line. Knute dashed

108

forward to block one of the halfbacks. But the Hamburg line stopped Red for a loss.

The Tigers were all looking worried. On last down Rudy called for a kick. Red barely had time to get the ball away. The Tigers couldn't stop the Hamburg boys, it seemed.

Now the Hamburg center passed the ball. The big Hamburg boys in the center of the line massed together and drove right over Al and Edgar and Otto. The ball carrier cut through behind them. He made a good gain before Red brought him down. Knute tried to slide in from the side to catch him from behind. But he was blocked out.

Down the field pounded the big Hamburg team. The crowd was all on their side. There were loud shouting and applause. The Tigers grew panicky as they were pushed back.

Finally Hamburg made a first down on the Tigers' twenty-yard line.

Edgar called for time out. The Tigers flopped on the ground, panting. Then they all tried to talk at once. Rudy was very excited. "We've got to stop them! We've got to stop them!"

Knute was worried. If the Tigers didn't settle down, they could never stop the Hamburg boys. He jumped up. "Hey, Rudy, I want to talk to you." He pulled Rudy aside. "Don't forget our crisscross play."

"Crisscross play?" Rudy snorted. "We haven't even got the ball!"

"Well, we'll get it," said Knute, "and when we do, we'll run right around 'em. Their halfbacks play in too close. You watch."

He sounded more confident than he felt. Rudy began to calm down as they walked back toward the rest of the team.

"We can stop them," Edgar was saying. "But we must charge low and hard."

Otto shook his head. He was discouraged.

The other boys got up, ready for play to begin. Otto just sat.

"Come on, Otto!" called Knute.

"Aw, I can't stop them," said Otto. "They walk right over me. I'm tired."

"What's the matter—are you afraid of them?" Knute knew Otto wasn't afraid. He just wanted to stir Otto up.

"What do you mean?" Otto forgot he was tired. He jumped up. "I'm not afraid of anything."

Knute shrugged his shoulders innocently.

The referee called time. The teams lined up. Just before the play, Knute darted over and gave Otto a good slap on the seat of the pants.

Otto charged forward, like a shot from a gun. He waded through two Hamburg blockers and threw the ball carrier for a big loss.

The Tigers all shouted and clapped Otto on the back. The Hamburg boys *could* be stopped.

The Tigers went back to their positions. They felt much more sure of themselves. They were no longer nervous.

"That's the way to stop them, Otto!" Knute cried.

Otto glanced suspiciously at Knute.

Knute grinned. "Sure, I was only kidding. You could lick any two of them."

Otto grinned back. "Maybe I was scared, at that!"

Back and forth the two teams struggled. Toward the end of the half, the Hamburg fullback finally broke through the Tiger line for a touchdown. Hamburg was ahead, 6-0.

Between halves the Tigers rested. At the beginning of the second half they started a drive down the field. On Hamburg's forty-yard line Rudy called for the crisscross play. He tossed the ball to Red. Red started around the right side of the line. The Hamburg boys swung over to get him. But he slipped the ball to Dick, who cut back sharply to the left. He got into the open and raced for the goal. Only the safety man was in his way. Knute tore down the field and blocked the safety man just in time. Dick scored a touchdown, and the score was tied.

After that, neither team could gain. With only a few minutes left, Edgar called time out.

"Our ball," said Rudy. "Let's break this tie!"

"Don't forget the triple pass," said Knute.

"I'm saving that for just the right time."

By turns Red and Dick and George Wolter carried the ball. Yard after yard they pushed slowly down the field. Time was running out. The Tigers were fighting hard to win. The Hamburg boys were battling to get the ball.

"Time for only one more play!" shouted the Hamburg captain.

Knute ran over to Rudy. "Aren't you going to use our triple pass?"

113

"This is the time," Rudy answered. "And it had better be good."

He rattled off the signals. He took the ball and handed it to Red. Red raced off to the left, but handed the ball to George. George cut back to the right.

"It's the crisscross play!" shouted the Hamburg captain. The orange sweaters all headed for George.

But George handed the ball to Knute. He hugged it and started back to the left as fast as he could run.

The Hamburg boys were completely fooled. Knute was nearly in the open, running hard for the goal. He dodged a halfback, and was in the clear. Only twenty yards to go!

"We're going to win!" thought Knute.

Suddenly he was horrified to see the crowd of boys and men rush onto the field in front of him.

"Get out of the way!" he shouted.

114

Before he knew what was happening, five or six boys dashed right toward him. He tried to get through, but they knocked him to the ground. Knute was furious! He fought to get up.

Now all the excited spectators ran onto the field. Somebody grabbed the ball from Knute.

A few men shouted, "Clear the field! Finish the game!"

All the players on both teams crowded around. The Tigers tried to get the ball. Fights started. The referee shouted, but nobody paid any attention to him.

At last Knute got to his feet. "Come on, fellows, I guess the game's over."

"It's not fair!" shouted Ferdy, as the Tigers picked up their street clothes and walked to their wagon. The others agreed loudly—but they climbed in and started home. As they left, policemen were still trying to clear the field.

Bumping along in their wagon, the Tigers were quiet for a long time. They felt pretty sad.

Finally Knute spoke up. "We should have had some of those boys in the crowd on our team. They're really rough!"

That struck the Tigers as funny. They began to cheer up.

116

Edgar said in a low voice to Red, "You know, Knute is pretty smart! He has a level head."

Red said, "Yes—I was surprised the way he calmed Rudy down and fired up Otto."

"Doggone it, I still say we should have won!" said Ferdy.

"There's nothing worse than a tie," Knute agreed. Then he grinned. "Anyway the triple pass worked!"

"They Won't Stop Me Now!"

Two YEARS later, when he was thirteen, Knute started to North West Division High School. Several of the Tigers entered the same school. They all wanted to try for the football team.

"I'll bet Otto makes it!" Knute prophesied, as he and Otto and Rudy turned into Claremont Street on the way to school. "The coaches won't let all that beef go to waste."

Otto playfully took a swing at Knute. Knute dodged and darted away. "Come on back," said Otto. "Better save your energy for football!"

"I'll miss Ferdy on the field. I wish he hadn't gone off to another school."

The boys departed to go to their classes. High school was new and strange to them. But they all saw a note on the bulletin board announcing football practice—that very afternoon! They wondered if they'd really have a chance to make the team. All the same, they showed up on the field after the last class.

Knute whistled in surprise. "Half the school must be here!"

"There's Mr. Peters," said Otto. "He teaches math, and he's one of the coaches."

"And here comes the other one. His name's Ellis. He's the physics teacher," said Rudy.

Mr. Ellis divided the new boys into groups. After a few exercises, he started them blocking and tackling. Then he walked around to size up all the newcomers.

Knute and Rudy and Otto charged and tackled as hard as they could. They wanted to make a good showing. Knute tore into Otto with a

119

flying tackle that sent him crashing to the ground.

"Hey!" Otto said. "It's not that important!"

"Yes, it is." Knute was determined to show the coaches what he could do.

For several days this went on. Then the boys had a chance to scrimmage. At the end of a week, the coaches passed out uniforms to those chosen for the team. As Knute had predicted, Otto made the team. Mr. Ellis went around and talked to each boy who had tried out. Some were told to try again next year. Some were allowed to stay on the scrubs.

Finally Mr. Ellis came to Knute. At his first question Knute's heart sank, because the coach asked, "How much do you weigh?"

"About a hundred and ten."

"H'mm," Mr. Ellis said.

Knute was on pins and needles. Was he too small? Why hadn't he grown more? Goodness knows, he ate enough! And exercised! What would Mr. Ellis say?

"Well, you're a fast runner," said Mr. Ellis. "Seems to me you ought to try out for track."

"I will," said Knute at once. "But I want to play football, too."

"This is a game for big fellows," Mr. Ellis said, "but since you're so eager, you can stay on the scrubs if you want to."

"I certainly do."

"It won't be much fun, unless you're crazy about the game. But it's good experience."

Knute was disappointed not to make the first eleven. But if he could just play—he'd get on the team yet! "That's fine with me."

"All right. I may not get much chance to coach you from now on. So I'll just show you a few things to start off. Here, take this ball." Mr. Ellis picked up a football and tossed it to Knute. "Now show me how you carry it."

"Why, like this." Knute tucked the ball under his arm.

"Run toward me," said the coach.

Knute started. Mr. Ellis stepped forward, reached out and hit the ball. It squirted right out of Knute's arms.

"Be sure to hold your hand over the end of the ball." Mr. Ellis smiled at Knute's embarrassment. "Everybody has to learn," he said.

"Now, then, get down into charging position. Suppose your side has the ball."

Knute crouched down. He got set. Mr. Ellis reached forward suddenly and gave Knute a hard push on the shoulders. Knute rolled over backward. He sat up, surprised.

The coach laughed. "You're not doing everything wrong," he said. "I think you're a fairly good tackler. But the best way to teach you is to let you see for yourself."

He showed Knute the correct charging posi-

122

tion, how to balance his weight firmly and solidly
—but be ready to drive in any direction.

At last he went on to the next boy.

Knute felt confused. How could he have been
so wrong? And the hours he had practiced to
play the game right! How would he ever get on
the team? "I thought I could play football," he
thought sadly. "I'll *really* have to work now."

And work he did. So did Rudy, who also was
on the scrubs. Knute practiced all the things Mr.
Ellis had shown him. He watched the team. He
listened to everything the coaches said. He
scrimmaged long and hard.

The scrubs were called in when the team was
learning a new play. Time after time the big
regulars would tear into them. Time after time
the scrubs would try to stop them. Knute
charged and tackled for all he was worth. Time
after time he picked himself up off the ground.
But he never got too much football.

When spring came, Knute went out for track. Though he was the smallest boy on the squad, he became the half-mile runner for North West Division High School. That summer, when he wasn't delivering papers or running errands, he was busy with baseball, tennis, running.

One afternoon, when the summer was nearly over, he was playing tennis in Humboldt Park with Johnny Devine. Johnny was on the track team with him.

"Game and set!" Knute called. He had rushed to the net and slammed the ball down the side line out of Johnny's reach.

"Good shot! How about one more set?"

"I told Otto we'd come over," answered Knute. "We'd better start."

The boys walked along Humboldt Boulevard, swinging their tennis rackets.

"Why don't you try out for football this fall?" Knute asked.

"Not me!" said Johnny. "I always end up at the bottom of the pile. But I like to watch."

"Want to go to the big high school game with me this fall?"

"What game is that?" Johnny asked.

"Why, the New York champion is coming here to play the Chicago champion!"

Johnny said, "How'll we get in?"

"We'd better begin saving for tickets right now. I have a new job lined up for this fall."

"What?" asked Johnny.

"Washing windows at the high school. Every Saturday morning. I'll get a cent and a half a window."

Just then they came to Otto's house. He was in the yard, practicing putting the shot.

"Hey, are you coming out for track next year?" Knute called.

"Maybe," said Otto. "But it's pretty hot for this today."

"Sit down, then, and watch Johnny and me practice starts!" Knute suggested.

Otto wiped his forehead. "You bet!"

Knute and Johnny crouched down, as if for the start of a race.

"On your mark—get set—*go!*" called Otto.

Knute and Johnny dashed forward, trying to see who could get off the mark quickest. Again and again they tried it.

"Whew!" sighed Johnny at last. "It *is* hot. I must rest for a minute."

Knute spied a clothes pole lying in the yard. "I'm going to try some pole vaulting," he said. "Maybe I'll be good enough for the team."

"Let's see you clear the fence," said Otto.

Knute got a good grip toward one end of the pole. He ran at top speed toward the fence, planted the end of the pole in the ground and vaulted neatly over the fence.

"Pretty good," said Johnny, "but it isn't high

enough. You'll have to go up about ten feet to make the team."

"I don't see anything here that high," said Knute. "I'll try the fence again."

Over he went again, but this time the pole cracked. Knute just missed falling.

"Doggone it!" he said, as he examined the pole. "Now I'll have to do something else."

"Since you have so much energy, why don't you try putting the shot?" Otto asked.

"I have a better idea. I just thought of a good exercise. It will strengthen my arms for pole vaulting. And for football, too."

Knute climbed the fence. On the top rail he crouched, grasped the rail firmly and slowly raised one leg and then the other until he was standing on his hands. Carefully he balanced himself. With his feet waving in the air to hold his balance, Knute walked up and down the fence on his hands!

128

"Doesn't he ever stop?" Johnny asked.

Otto laughed. "I've never seen him stop yet."

Knute let his feet down and dropped from the fence to the ground. "Well I must stop now and carry my papers. See you at the tennis court tomorrow, Johnny?" Knute ran down the street toward home.

A few months later, in November, Johnny and Knute pushed their way through the crowd into the bleachers at the big Chicago-New York high school football game.

On the field cheerleaders were doing stunts. The teams hadn't come out yet.

"I bet you wish you were playing today," said Johnny.

"Oh, I guess so." But Knute didn't sound very eager.

Johnny looked at him in amazement. "What's the matter with you today? I thought you were crazy about football!"

"Sure I am, but maybe Coach Ellis is right. He says I'm too small for the team."

"Oh, you'll grow!"

"Well, another season's over, and I've been on the scrubs two years," said Knute sadly. "Maybe I ought to stick to track."

Johnny laughed. "You can't fool me! You won't give up until you make the team."

Knute shook his head. "I wonder if I ever will."

The crowd jumped up and cheered. From one side of the field came the Brooklyn Poly Prep team, champion of New York. From the other came the Hyde Park High School team, champion of Chicago.

"Looks bad for Hyde Park," Knute said.

"Yes, those Brooklyn boys are giants."

"See the Chicago quarterback!" said Knute. "That must be Walter Eckersall. He's their star player—but he isn't much bigger than I am!"

Knute reached into his pocket for his program. "Why, Eckersall weighs only a hundred and twenty!" He stared at the black-haired, stocky boy in surprise.

The teams took their places for the kickoff. Knute and Johnny both yelled for Hyde Park. But Knute thought the Chicago boys wouldn't stand a chance. They were outweighed at least ten pounds a man. It would be a walkaway for Brooklyn, he was sure.

131

Brooklyn kicked off—a low, hard kick that carried almost to the goal. Eckersall raced over and caught the ball. He dashed down the field. The Brooklyn boys swarmed up the field after him. Three or four tried to tackle him. But he twisted and turned and brought the ball almost to the fifty-yard line.

"Look how he straight-armed that halfback!" shouted Knute.

The teams lined up. Eckersall barked out his signals. His voice rang clear and sharp all over the field. Eckersall pretended to give the ball to the fullback. Instead he tossed it to the halfback who circled wide around the end. Eckersall led the interference. A big Brooklyn halfback rushed up to stop the play. Eckersall plowed into him like an express train. "He certainly hits hard," Knute marveled. The Hyde Park halfback carried the ball for a twenty-yard gain.

On the next play Eckersall gave the ball to the

fullback. The fullback charged right through the Brooklyn line for another good gain.

"Watch that blocking, Johnny," said Knute. "Those Hyde Park boys are perfect! They're shoving that Brooklyn team right off the field!"

There was Eckersall calling his signals again. He seemed always to call the play that Brooklyn didn't expect. The Hyde Park team moved like clockwork. Each player carried out his assignment perfectly.

"Why—why—it's beautiful!" said Knute, his eyes wide in astonishment. "I never saw football like this before."

Down the field went Hyde Park for a touchdown. Then Brooklyn got the ball.

They tried a mass play, right over center. The Brooklyn linemen charged close together. It looked as though the smaller Chicago boys would be swept aside. But they held. They dug their feet firmly in the ground. They drove low and hard. They upset the Brooklyn linemen and stopped the runner right at the line of scrimmage, without a gain.

Knute got more excited with each play. He could hardly believe his eyes. He watched everything the Chicago players did. Why couldn't he play that way? He vowed he would!

Hyde Park got the ball again. Once again Eckersall's voice rang out. Play after play the Chicago boys executed with wonderful precision—for another touchdown.

"That's the way football should be played," Knute shouted. "Every man knows exactly what to do on every play."

"They just have good players," said Johnny.

"That isn't all," said Knute. "Look how they block! Look how they tackle! Look at their teamwork! Their coach has taught them plenty. He must know a lot about football."

The game turned into a rout. When it was

over, Eckersall and his Hyde Park teammates had beaten Brooklyn, 105-0.

Knute was on fire with enthusiasm. Never had he imagined such a football game!

"Did I say something about quitting football?" Knute exclaimed on the way home. "From now on, my middle name is Eckersall! They won't stop me now!"

Knute Is Downhearted

THE CROWD roared. People swarmed all over the football field.

Knute tore off his headgear. He rushed up and thumped Otto on the back. The other players crowded around and congratulated one another. North West Division had just beaten a powerful Marshall High School team. And Knute was playing regular right end.

It was his last year in high school. After three seasons on the scrubs, he had made the team.

"Crane Tech next week," said one of the boys.

"And then North Division," shouted Otto.

"What a schedule!" said Knute, as he walked

back to the dressing room with them. "Two of the toughest teams in Chicago."

"That's right," Otto said. "I hope we can play them the way we played Marshall today!"

Knute saw his father standing on the side line. He ran over to him. "I didn't know you were coming today, Pa."

"I managed to find some free time," said Mr. Rockne. "I saw part of the game. You played well, son."

"Thanks, Pa. I'm glad you came."

"I'll have to admit, football *is* exciting!"

During the next week, the team practiced hard for the game with Crane Technical High School. On Wednesday Knute got his report card for the first weeks of the term. When he looked at it, his heart sank. "Oh," he said to himself, "what's happened to my grades?"

He had barely passed in two subjects. He had received only a fair grade in the other two.

Knute was disturbed. He knew he could do better. "Well, I'll just have to make it up after football season is over," he thought. Maybe he ought to study more now. Maybe——

"Hurry up, Knute!" called Otto. "Get out to practice."

Knute put the card in his pocket as he joined Otto. Walking down the hall, they met Johnny. "Hey, Knute," he called. "Did you hear about the indoor track meets this winter?"

"No, what's this all about?"

"There are a lot of meets scheduled. I think we could enter most of them. Then we'd be in great shape for the team next spring."

"Field events, too?" Knute asked.

"Pole vault and everything!" said Johnny.

Knute thought a minute. "I'd certainly like to if I ever get caught up with my schoolwork."

"Huh!" Otto said. "You're smart. You won't have any trouble with that."

138

"Anyway," said Knute, "right now we have some football trouble on our hands. Thanks for telling me about the track meets, Johnny."

"Good luck against Crane!" said Johnny.

North West had a bitter battle with Crane. Knute and his team fought hard, for Crane was favored to win. The game finally ended in a tie.

"Whew!" Otto said later. "That was a tough game. And North Division is supposed to be even tougher."

"Well, we showed Crane they couldn't walk over us," Knute declared. "But I hate a tie game. It reminds me of our game with Hamburg."

Otto laughed. "Don't you ever forget a game?"

"Well, I remember how our triple pass worked against their defense," Knute said. "Details like that may come in handy!"

North Division proved just as good as its reputation. North West Division fought hard, but lost by a small margin. It was their only loss of the season.

With football over for the year, Knute and Johnny gave most of their attention to the indoor track meets. Knute just couldn't resist them. Especially now that he had gone in for pole vaulting. Somehow, his good resolutions about studying were pushed into the background.

One day the following spring he suggested to Johnny that they go over to Humboldt Park for a workout. "I have a study period," Knute said. "A bunch of fellows have already started over."

"We'd better get permission from Mr. Kopp," said Johnny.

They looked all over for the gym teacher, but they couldn't find him.

"Shall we go anyway?" Knute asked.

"Well, he always lets the track team practice during study hours," said Johnny.

Knute hesitated. "Maybe it wouldn't hurt if

we don't have permission just this once. Let's go! We haven't much time."

"North West ought to do pretty well in track this spring," Johnny said as the boys hurried along. "You're getting good in the half mile—you might even break the record this year."

"Well, you're plenty fast yourself!"

"Are you going to run on the Chicago Athletic Association team this year, too?"

"If they'll let me," Knute said. "But what I'm really looking forward to is college this fall. I'm going to Chicago University, you know."

"You might get on the same football team with Eckersall. I'm glad we saw him. Now he's the star player for Chicago—and an All-American!"

"I'll never forget him," Knute said. "Say, Johnny, are you going to college?"

"I'm thinking about going to Notre Dame."

"Notre Dame? Where's that?"

"Why, in South Bend, Indiana."

"I never heard of it," said Knute. "Have they got a football team?"

"Have they! And the best part is, there are plenty of jobs if you want to work your way. Waiting tables, and things like that. And part-time jobs in South Bend."

"That is a big help," Knute answered.

The boys reached Humboldt Park. Several members of the North West track team were already running and jumping. Johnny and Knute practiced starts, then jogged a few laps.

"How about letting me check your time?" asked Johnny.

"You bet. Will you hold the watch?"

"I've got it here," Johnny said.

Knute knelt down at the starting line.

"On your mark—get set—go!"

Knute dashed away. He hoped he *could* break the record this spring. He was feeling good. He paced himself carefully. Gradually he speeded up. He lunged for the finish line, straining every muscle.

"Two minutes and two seconds!" Johnny called. Knute trotted back, panting hard. "That's the best you've done. You'll break the record sure."

Knute grinned. "I felt like running today. Want me to time you now?"

Before Johnny could answer, they heard a sharp voice behind them. "Boys! What are you doing here in school hours?"

Knute, Johnny, and the other boys looked up. There stood Mr. Fiske, the school principal.

Knute spoke up. "Why, Mr. Fiske, we're practicing for the track team."

"Do you have permission to be here?"

Knute stuttered. "Why—why—we couldn't find Mr. Kopp. But he always lets us practice during study period. And—and—I thought it wouldn't hurt today."

"Do any of you boys have permission?" Mr. Fiske asked.

Nobody answered. "This is awful!" thought Knute.

Mr. Fiske cleared his throat. "There's been far too much of this going on lately. You know, you can't compete on teams unless you keep up your classwork and follow the regulations of the school."

He hesitated a minute. "Boys," he went on, "I'm sorry to do this, but I feel I must set an example. You are all dismissed from school, and may not return."

"But, Mr. Fiske——"

"I'm sorry, Knute," said Mr. Fiske. "You're one of our bright boys. But your marks have suffered from too much athletics."

Knute's heart sank. Mr. Fiske sounded just like Pa. What would Pa say? Knute felt worse and worse.

144

"After a period of suspension, I will arrange your transfers to other schools," Mr. Fiske said. "I know this is harsh, but it is necessary." He walked away.

None of the boys said anything. Slowly Knute leaned down to pick up his coat.

Johnny finally found his voice. "It isn't fair! We didn't do anything *that* wrong!"

The other boys agreed.

"It does seem stiff," Knute said. "But I guess Mr. Fiske is right, too."

He walked home slowly with Johnny. Neither boy felt like talking. Knute was thinking, "Maybe I did let my work slide. But I always passed."

At last he said aloud, "Gee, Johnny, what can we do about it?"

"Nothing, I guess. We didn't really get permission to go over there."

They came to Knute's house. Knute couldn't help smiling a little. "Johnny, you look as bad as

I feel. Cheer up! Maybe we'll both get to college yet."

Supper was very quiet at the Rockne house that night. After the meal, Pa took Knute into the front room alone.

Mr. Rockne paced up and down. "Knute," he said, "I can understand about your not getting permission. Yes, yes, indeed. You were wrong, but that really didn't matter greatly."

146

Knute felt a bit better.

"But this does show me you're more serious about athletics than studying," his father went on. "I have been distressed by your lack of attention to your schoolwork. Knute, you've wasted your opportunities! You've been so crazy about sports you've thought of nothing else."

"But, Pa——"

"Now, don't misunderstand me. I've been proud of your accomplishments. That's why I've gone to track meets and games to watch you. But you remember what I told you—there can be too much athletics."

"I'm sure I can make up my work!" Knute protested. "I wouldn't let it happen again!"

"I'm afraid it's too late. Knute, I can't send you to college. It wouldn't be fair to the girls. They have to have their chance. It's hard for me to say it—but I can't spend the money on someone who doesn't appreciate opportunities."

Anne came into the room. "Pa, Knute ought to go to college. Really, he ought. We girls won't mind!"

"Now, Anne," said her father, "your loyalty is very fine. But this is between Knute and me."

"All right, Pa." Anne went to the door.

Mr. Rockne turned to his son. "I'm sorry, Knute. My mind is made up. You'd better look for a job immediately. If you are really determined to continue your education, you'll find your own way."

"Maybe I have been doing too much," Knute thought. Yes, he'd admit that. "If I only had one more chance!"

But now that he couldn't go to school he knew he wanted to finish his education. Why, he really liked to study! He'd have to find a way.

In their room, his mother and father were talking.

"Oh, Lars," she said, "don't you think we

ought to send Knute to college? Why, you had your heart set on it!"

Mr. Rockne walked up and down. "Martha, when things come too easily, they're not always appreciated. Knute must learn to value his education. Then, I'm sure, he'll really work for it."

"But you know he has a good mind. We ought to help him get ahead."

"I won't send him to college just to play games. Not when the girls need schooling, too." Mr. Rockne paused. "Maybe it seems harsh. But I think it's the fairest thing to Knute himself."

"How do you mean?"

"He's a very independent boy. And that's right. He's growing up. I tried to warn him not to lose his head over sports. Now he'll have to decide for himself what he wants. Perhaps that's the only way he'll really learn."

"But I'm sure he'd make up this work."

Mr. Rockne sighed. "Martha, Scandinavians

149

are stubborn men. This will be a hard lesson for Knute, but it's up to him to prove himself now. If he's determined, it will be hard to stop him. Only time will tell. We'll have to wait and see."

Time did tell. For four years Knute worked in the Chicago post office. He saved his money. In the fall of 1910 he finally went to college—to Notre Dame. And Johnny Devine was right: Knute was able to earn much of his way by waiting tables and doing other part-time jobs.

Dorais to
Rockne

THE SUN was low in the sky over blue Lake Erie.
At the summer resort of Cedar Point, in Ohio,
the crowd was beginning to leave the beach.
Soon it would be dinnertime at the popular
Breakers Hotel.

The few men in the lake began to swim in.
Several little girls were still wading in the shallow water. Some boys were still playing ball on
the beach. But ladies were closing their parasols
and calling to the children.

Standing apart, with watchful eyes on the
swimmers, were two sunburned young men. On
their bathing suits were the words Life Guard.

A man who had been sunbathing noticed them as he stood up and brushed off the sand. He remarked, "Cedar Point usually hires life guards with more muscle."

"I guess these are strong enough," said the man beside him. "They told me they're football players. From the University of Notre Dame in Indiana."

"Those boys? Why, neither one can weigh more than 140 pounds. The 1913 football season will be sad for Notre Dame!"

"Yes—and I understand they're going to play Army this year."

"Well, that'll be just a warm-up game for West Point. What positions do the boys play?"

"The stocky one is the quarterback—Gus Dorais. The other plays end. He's captain of the team, too. His name's Knute Rockne."

The life guard with husky shoulders and spindly legs didn't see the two men staring at him. He walked over to Gus Dorais. "It's time to go off duty, and the last swimmer is out of the water. Have you got the football?"

"Sure—under my sweater over there."

"Bring it up to the end of the beach." Knute scuffed through the deep white sand toward the water. Where the breakers rolled in, the wet sand was smooth and hard-packed.

He was thinking about a problem. In September his last year at Notre Dame would begin. Soon he must decide how he would earn his living. What was he going to do? Would Father Cavanaugh offer him a teaching job at Notre Dame? The president of the university had once hinted at that.

Knute was glad things had worked out so that he had gone to Notre Dame instead of Chicago University, as Pa had planned. He wished Pa were still alive to see him graduate with honors. Pa would have been so proud. But if Knute upheld his record as a star athlete, too, he'd need all the practice he could get. His team had a hard football season ahead. That was why he and Gus spent all their spare time practicing. They were working now on the forward pass.

When Gus joined him, Knute said eagerly, "I was watching some kids play baseball today, and I got an idea. There ought to be a way to put more arm action into the forward pass. That's what gives speed and accuracy to a baseball throw. You can use your whole arm, because you can get a good grip on a baseball."

Gus nodded. "But with something the shape of a football, all you can do is lay it on your palm and heave it."

"Well, I thought today: why couldn't we grip the football right near the end instead of around the thickest part?" He took the ball and showed Gus the grip he meant. Then he half turned, drew back his arm and threw the ball.

154

It whipped through the air and dropped far down the beach. Gus dashed after it. When he brought it back he said, "Golly, Knute, with that grip you aren't just lobbing it. You'll be able to control your throw. Let's try it."

Knute ran down the beach a distance. Gus rifled a pass toward him. Knute got ready to catch it up against his chest. The ball came straight toward him. Even Knute was surprised to see how accurate the throw had been. He returned the ball—and it went right into Gus's arms. The boys passed to each other several times.

They both grew excited.

"Say, this is swell!" Gus shouted. "I can throw a spiral every time. The ball doesn't wobble in the air. I'll be able to place it right where we want it."

Knute came closer. "It'll make the forward pass a real threat. And here for months I've been trying to see a way to perfect the pass. It's been allowed under the rules for seven years but only a few teams have used it. They never could get much power into it. But now if we can control the direction and length of the pass——"

"It'll be a great offensive play!" Gus interrupted excitedly. "And will it surprise Army!"

"You bet. We can spread out their defense with passes. Then when they're expecting another you can send Pliska or Eichenlaub through the line. We'll get Army so mixed up they won't know what to expect!" Knute began to back away. "Throw me another one now, Gus," he added. "Right into my hands!"

The boys practiced short passes. Then Gus called, "Let's try a longer one. Get back farther. Ready? Here it comes—Dorais to Rockne!"

He arched a long pass into the air. Knute saw at once that Gus had misjudged. The ball would drop in the water. He raced after it. Without slowing, he reached up and grabbed the ball with his fingertips.

"Hey, nice catch!" Gus called.

Knute ran down the beach toward him. "Say —why couldn't I catch 'em that way—running— every time? Do I have to catch a ball in my arms, against my chest? It means I must always stop and wait for the ball. I'm an easy target for any tackler."

Gus was thinking fast. "There's more chance of dropping the ball——"

"Not if I practice enough," Knute argued. "I could improve my catching until it would be a sure thing."

Gus laughed. "We'll be tossing the pigskin around like a baseball."

"Right! Now let's get busy." Knute ran back down the beach.

Gus counted, "One-two-three." He faded back, whirled, raised his arm and threw.

Knute ran forward. Again he reached out and caught the ball in his hands without slowing up.

Over and over they practiced the play. Long passes, short passes, passes from all angles. "A few more off to the left now," Knute suggested.

Gus shook his head firmly. "What's the use of perfecting the pass if we starve to death before we meet Army? I'm quitting for supper, and so are you!"

On the afternoon of November 1, 1913, fifteen Notre Dame players trotted onto the football field at West Point, New York. The big Army squad was already on the gridiron. Several full teams were charging and kicking and running. The stands were filled with cadets in gray uniforms.

On the side lines, newspapermen were watching. One remarked, "This will be a walkaway for Army. Only fifteen Notre Dame players! And they're outweighed fifteen pounds a man."

158

"I hear they have a very open style of play," said another. "But they'll need more than that against Army."

"Army's got McEwen at center, Merrillat at end and Pritchard at quarterback. Three All-Americans. They'll murder Notre Dame."

Out on the field, the Notre Dame eleven huddled together with Coach Jess Harper. "All right, men," he said. "You know what to do. It's our first big eastern appearance, and it means a lot to Notre Dame. Go get 'em!"

They ran to their positions. Army kicked off. Ray Eichenlaub, Notre Dame's fullback and biggest man, brought the ball back to the thirty-yard line.

"Signals!" barked Gus Dorais. He called for Pliska, the right halfback, to carry the ball off tackle. Notre Dame gained three yards.

Dorais called his next signal. Knute grinned. It was their forward pass.

The ball was snapped. Knute cut down field. Gus started out as though he were going to run with the ball. Suddenly he stopped and threw a bulletlike spiral.

Still running, Knute looked back over his shoulder. The ball was coming. He reached up and caught it with his finger tips. Before he could run, Pritchard tackled him. But it was a twenty-yard gain. First down, Notre Dame!

There was a wave of excitement in the stands. Nobody had ever seen a pass like that—or such a catch—before.

"Dorais to Rockne. Well, what do you think of that?" one reporter exclaimed. "Maybe these Notre Dame boys have something, after all!"

Dorais called for Eichenlaub to plunge. Then for Pliska to run. Then he threw another pass to Knute. Notre Dame was pushing the big Army team toward its goal.

"Let's lick these Hoosiers!" Merrillat yelled to

160

the Army players. The cadets in the stands shouted, "Hold that line! Hold that line!"

At the fifteen-yard line, Notre Dame was stopped. It was last down, five yards to go.

The teams lined up.

The Army captain shouted, "It'll be another pass. Watch out for Rockne!"

Dorais called the signal. It *was* a pass. Knute ran toward the goal. Two Army men were close on his heels, ready to intercept the ball.

Knute headed for the corner of the field. Dorais threw. The ball arched ahead of Knute, high in the air. With every ounce of strength he had, he leaped in the air, above the outstretched hands of the Army players. He snared the ball, and fell over the goal for a touchdown. Notre Dame led, 6-0!

"You never ran better in your life!" Pliska told Knute. The other players clapped him on the back. The crowd was cheering.

Knute called to Gus as they ran to take their positions, "Our Life Guard special. I told you practice would pay off."

Gus grinned back. Then he calmly kicked the extra point. Notre Dame led, 7-0.

But the Army team was aroused. They took the kickoff and fought back grimly.

They pounded the Notre Dame line. Yard by yard, they plowed down the field. Knute kept cheering his players on. Notre Dame charged furiously. They tackled hard. But Army was not to be denied. Fullback Hodgson charged over for a touchdown!

Once again Army got the ball. Once again the West Pointers started a march down the field. From the ten-yard line, All-American Pritchard slashed over for another touchdown. Captain Hoge kicked the extra point, and the score was: Army 13, Notre Dame 7.

Knute called his players around him. "They're

outflanking us. Play a little wider in the line."
Then the whisle blew for the kickoff.

"Fellows," said Captain Rockne, "when the going gets tough, that's when we like it. Let's get that ball, and go, go, go!"

Notre Dame started to move. Eichenlaub smashed for yardage. Knute caught another pass for a gain. Pliska circled the end and picked up more yards. Down the field they went. As they got closer to the goal, Army's defense grew stiffer. Again it was last down for Notre Dame.

Knute winked at Gus. Dorais called signals.

Knute darted down the field, waving his arms to Gus to throw him the ball. The Army players didn't realize the signal was too obvious—a trick. They rushed over to tackle Knute.

Dorais calmly whirled and threw the ball to Pliska, who raced over for a touchdown. The half ended: Notre Dame 14, Army 13.

When the second half started, the West Pointers battled hard to hold Notre Dame. They smashed furiously down the field, but neither team scored in the third quarter.

Knute told Gus, "A one-point lead is too slim. We must surprise Army."

On the next play Dorais called for a pass. Knute started down the field, but he was limping badly. Dorais threw to Pliska for a short gain.

On the Notre Dame bench a substitute exclaimed, "Rockne's hurt!"

The coach jumped up, worried. Then he smiled and sat down again. "He's not hurt—he's only acting. He always thinks of something."

For several plays Knute kept on limping. Dorais didn't throw the ball to him once. The Army defenders began to watch Pliska steadily. Dorais was passing to him for short gains. They didn't pay any attention to Knute.

Dorais called still another pass. Suddenly Knute sprinted at top speed straight down the field. Dorais threw the ball right into his arms. Knute caught it on the run and headed for the goal. Pritchard finally tackled him, but Notre Dame was deep in Army territory.

In three smashes Eichenlaub carried the ball over for a touchdown. Dorais kicked goal. Notre Dame 21, Army 13.

Notre Dame got the ball again. Dorais called his plays skillfully—passes when Army expected line plunges, end runs when Army expected passes. Pliska made another touchdown, Eichenlaub still another.

The crowd in the stands had gone wild. The cadets were hoarse from yelling. The reporters were amazed. "Army is baffled," said one.

"Nobody knows what'll happen next," another said. "Why, this kind of play could change the whole game of football!"

Army was still fighting hard. They used forward passes, trying to score. But Pritchard's throws were wobbly and uncertain, and Army could not gain.

The gun sounded. Notre Dame had beaten Army, 35-13!

The Notre Dame boys hugged one another. They rushed to congratulate the Army team.

The Army coach walked across the field to Coach Harper. "You have a great team," he said. He talked earnestly for several minutes.

Coach Harper nodded. "Rockne! Dorais!"

"Pritchard! Merrillat!" called Coach Daly.

The two quarterbacks and the two ends trotted up to the Notre Dame bench.

Coach Harper said, "Knute, will you and Gus explain our forward passing? Coach Daly would like to use it against Navy."

Knute grinned. To think that he and Gus could teach All-Americans about football! "Sure," he said. He and Gus gave the Army players a demonstration.

"That Dorais is a marvel," the Army coach remarked.

"Yes, he is," Coach Harper agreed. "There aren't many like him. But Rockne's the fellow who worked out the technique and the plays."

Just then Pritchard threw a nice spiral.

"Look, he's getting the hang of it!" said the Army coach. "Rockne must be a good teacher, too."

"Yes, he is! He knows how to put his ideas across to the boys," said Coach Harper. "He's going to be my assistant next year—if I can persuade him."

Rockne of
Notre Dame

It was November 20, 1920. The cheers of a crowd filled the stadium. The scoreboard read Notre Dame 22, Northwestern 7.

The pistol shot rang out to end the game. The crowd began to spill down onto the field. The teams headed for their dressing rooms.

Up in the stands a man wearing the blue and gold colors of Notre Dame turned to another alumnus. In a voice hoarse from yelling he said, "I never saw a halfback like George Gipp!"

"He's certainly Notre Dame's greatest. Perhaps one of the greatest who ever lived."

As they waited their chance to get out, the first

man said, "But not even an All-American like Gipp can beat a team like Northwestern single-handed. It takes a whole team—plus Knute Rockne."

"Mostly Rockne! Why, since he became head coach Notre Dame is almost unbeatable! It hasn't lost a game in those two years! He's a wizard!"

"Coaches and sports writers all over the country say he's changing the whole game of football with his Notre Dame system."

Meanwhile, in the dressing rooms newspapermen had surrounded the team.

"Oh, Rock," one called, "will you give us a story?"

"Be glad to in a minute," said the round-faced, stocky man. "As soon as I see if my boys are all right."

Rockne walked around the room where the trainers were busy with the players.

"How's that shoulder, Chet? Be sure to get some heat on it."

To one of the halfbacks he said, "Nice game, Norm. You looked good out there. You drove hard, and you stayed on your feet."

One reporter remarked, "No wonder Rock's kids love him—he takes a personal interest in every boy. We won't see him until he's talked to everyone who played."

After the coach had made the rounds he came back to the newspapermen. "Sorry to keep you waiting, but those boys have just played a hard game."

"Rock, the experts are picking Notre Dame for the national champion this year. Think you'll make it?"

Knute smiled broadly. "Better ask the boys. They're the ones to do it!"

"How about next year? Another unbeaten season?"

"We'll lose a lot of boys who graduate, you know. You answer the question. Can any team go on winning forever? We'll probably lose several games next year."

One reporter laughed. "The same Rockne story. You told us that at the start of this season!"

Knute chuckled. "Did I? I don't remember it. But, you know, every now and then a defeat is good for a team. It keeps them from thinking they're *too* good." He hesitated a moment. "But," he added, "*too* many defeats aren't good for the coach."

The reporters laughed. "No danger of your losing your job," said one. "Notre Dame will never let you go!"

"What's your secret?" asked another. "Why are your teams so successful?"

"We haven't any secret," answered Rockne, "except maybe hard practice. Come around next year and watch us!"

It was the next fall. The reporters had returned to watch Notre Dame practice. They stood on the side lines. Several hundred boys in uniforms were divided into groups. They took turns charging at one another. Their cleated shoes churned up the turf as they drove hard. Coach Rockne walked about, giving pointers.

A young reporter pushed his hat to the back of his head. "This looks like any other blocking drill. What makes Notre Dame so good?"

One of the older men smiled. "It may look like any other, but it isn't! Rockne teaches his boys to do everything just a little better than anyone else. Haven't you heard his motto: 'Practice, practice, practice! Practice makes perfect, and perfect practice makes a winning team'?"

The coach came to a group close to the side lines. One player was trying a block. He charged in slowly and halfheartedly.

"What's the matter, Bill?" Knute asked.

"Think this is a tea party? Let's see you drive! And do it fast. Otherwise you'll ruin a play someday! Look here!"

Knute himself dropped into position and charged. Bill was a huge boy, weighing at least 225 pounds. He tried to push Rockne away, but Knute bobbed his head, dodged the outstretched arms, and hooked his shoulder into the boy's side.

"That's what I mean, Bill. If an old man like me can do it, you surely can!"

Bill looked sheepish. He tried again. This time he charged in energetically. He made a good block.

"Now you're getting the idea!"

Rockne walked off to the center of the field. His assistant blew a whistle.

"Everybody up here!" the coach called. "Let's see how you look in scrimmage. But remember, I want you to keep blocking and tackling. If you can't block and tackle, you can't play football.

174

You should love to block! Remember, football is a game—and you ought to get fun out of it! And the fun comes when you learn to play it right.

"All right, now! 'A' team has the ball. First and ten on their own forty. Let's look alive now! Play ball!"

He and his assistants went to the side lines. The "A" team and the "B" team ran off several plays.

"Hold it!" yelled Rockne. "We'll run that same play four times." To a halfback he said, "Joe, you're giving it away every time. Why don't you send the other team a post card?"

The other boys grinned.

Rockne continued, "Look straight ahead until the ball is snapped. Then move—and fast! After all, the object of a good offense is surprise!"

The quarterback called the same play until Rockne was satisfied.

After practice the reporters followed **Knute** to his office.

"We didn't see much passing this afternoon," said one. "Are you going to stay with a running game this season?"

Rockne shook his head. "We can run," he said, "but we can pass, too. We try to do everything well—then the other team doesn't know what to expect."

In the office another reporter spoke up. "We've seen a lot of fine athletes today. They're working hard under good direction. But we can see that on a hundred practice fields. What makes the difference, Rock? What keeps Notre Dame on top?"

Rockne looked out the window. "You haven't seen my first assistant," he said. He nodded toward a priest who was walking by. "That's Father John O'Hara, the Prefect of Religion. I try to keep the boys fit on the playing field. Father O'Hara keeps them fit in his much more important department. I wish I could do my job half as well as he does his."

"What do you look for in a boy, Rock?"

Knute thought a minute. "Hard work," he said. "I expect my boys to be smart in the classroom, and they must be clever on the football field. I look for them to be quick of wit, to have a sense of humor and to play fair. They all know my three rules: shoot square, live clean and never make excuses. It all takes work. But I don't know of a better way for a boy to spend his time."

"Football's only a game. Why do you demand such perfection?"

"There's no satisfaction in doing any job halfway."

The newspapermen nodded.

"And another thing," Knute continued: "I want our athletic standards to equal the high scholastic standards of the university."

On January 1, 1925, the Notre Dame football team trotted out on a sunny field. They were competing in the Rose Bowl game in Pasadena, California. Fifty-two thousand people rose and cheered. It would be the greatest game of the season—unbeaten Stanford against unbeaten Notre Dame.

"Whew! It's hot today," said a spectator. "The Irish won't find it easy to play their best game when they're used to cold weather. But I'm rooting for them."

"They won't be able to stop Ernie Nevers," said his companion, who had graduated from Stanford. "What a fullback!"

"Well, what about the Four Horsemen?" the Notre Dame man wanted to know. "They're the greatest backfield in the history of the game."

His friend laughed. "Some name for a backfield!"

"Wait'll they ride all over Stanford! Then

you won't laugh. Remember, they have the Seven Mules in the line to lead the way."

The Stanford man was still joking about the nicknames when the game got under way.

Rockne started his second team. Stanford took the ball down the field. Powerful Ernie Nevers drove through the Notre Dame line. But near the goal Notre Dame held firm. Stanford kicked a field goal. The quarter ended: Stanford 3, Notre Dame 0.

Then Rockne sent in his first team—the Four Horsemen and the Seven Mules. The crowd roared as eleven new men trotted onto the field. Almost at once Notre Dame began to move forward. Their plays were perfectly executed. They made one first down after another.

The Four Horsemen lived up to their reputation. Elmer Layden streaked around end. Don Miller dashed off tackle. Jimmy Crowley threw a beautiful pass. And every play Harry Stuhldreher called seemed to hit a weak spot in the Stanford team. Then Layden went across for a touchdown.

While Stanford took time out, the Stanford man up in the stands said, "Just you wait! The game's not over."

The Notre Dame man chuckled. "I can wait."

"Still, I must admit I've never seen more beautiful teamwork. They're so smooth! And those Four Horsemen weigh only about a hundred and fifty-eight apiece. How did Rockne ever find such marvelous players?"

"Well, Don Miller was a third-string high-school player. Layden was a good punter and could run fast—but lots of players can punt and run. Crowley could pass pretty well, but he was the sleepiest-looking fellow you ever saw. And Harry Stuhldreher was as slow as molasses."

"Don't try to kid me!"

"It's the truth. Then they got together under

Rockne. If they're smooth now, it's because Rock showed them the way to work. And, boy, are they good!"

"Here they go again!"

Stanford got the ball and started down the field. Nevers gained ground time after time. Then the Stanford quarterback called for a forward pass. He threw it out to the side. Like a cat, Layden of Notre Dame pounced on the ball. He caught it right out of a Stanford man's arms, and raced down the field. Jimmy Crowley charged in front of him, knocking Stanford players out of the way. Layden ran seventy yards for a touchdown!

The Stanford fans groaned.

On the side lines, Knute Rockne sighed with relief. "Just what we were waiting for!"

In the press box, a Los Angeles reporter threw down his pencil in disgust. "That Notre Dame bunch is the luckiest team I've ever seen!"

"Luck?" said a reporter from Chicago. "Why, when I was in South Bend a while ago, I saw the team practice that very play. Rockne was expecting Stanford to try just such a pass. He had Layden prepared for it. It's hard practice that makes luck."

When the half ended the score was: Notre Dame 13, Stanford 3.

"Wait till the second half," said the Los Angeles reporter. "Those small Notre Dame men can't stand up long against Stanford."

"Don't forget the Notre Dame shift. Didn't you notice how the backfield moves to one side or the other before each play? That way, a small man can get the jump on a big man. Rockne would rather have a fast, small man than a slow, big one every time. Size is not so important."

When the second half started, Notre Dame couldn't gain. Layden punted. There was a fumble. Hunsinger, the Notre Dame end, scooped up the ball. He raced for a touchdown. Notre Dame 20, Stanford 3.

"I suppose Notre Dame practiced *that* play?" the reporter sneered.

"Well, Rockne's teams are trained to be alert every minute!"

The stadium was in an uproar. Then the Stanford team got started. Nevers plowed through the Notre Dame line. Stanford scored a touchdown. Notre Dame 20, Stanford 10.

Once again Stanford got the ball. They roared down the field. By this time the Notre Dame men were beginning to feel the heat. Nevers gained yards every time he carried the ball.

Then the Stanford quarterback called for a pass: the same pass out to the side. Once again, Layden grabbed the ball. Crowley ran interference. Layden raced sixty-five yards for another touchdown.

All the spectators were on their feet, shouting

at the spectacular play. Notre Dame had struck again—like lightning!

On the bench Rockne said, "I never thought they'd repeat that pass. I'm glad we were ready."

Still Stanford was not beaten. They took heart and strove for victory. Notre Dame was tiring. Stanford made first down close to the goal. On the second down they reached the three-yard line.

The Notre Dame players were worried. "How'll we stop them?" asked one. "Why doesn't Rock tell us?"

"Here comes a substitute! He'll have a message!" said another.

One more play was run. Stanford reached the two-yard line. Almost a touchdown!

Now the team could crowd around the substitute. "What did Rock tell you? What'll we do?"

The substitute grinned. "Rock says for you to hold 'em!"

The Notre Dame players looked blank. Then they laughed. They no longer felt nervous. "So Rock thinks it's up to us," said Stuhldreher. "All right, we won't let him down!"

On the next play the Notre Dame linemen charged like fury. They stopped Stanford, and the ball went over to Notre Dame. Layden moved back to kick. The ball soared high and far down the field. It traveled eighty yards!

Up in the stands, the loyal Stanford fan sat down with a sigh. "You can't beat a team like that," he said sadly.

The game ended: Notre Dame 27, Stanford 10. Rockne had coached Notre Dame to a second national championship!

On the afternoon of December 6, 1930, a group of football fans were gathered around the radio at the University Club in Chicago.

"What a game this'll be!" said a man who had attended Notre Dame. "The Irish against Southern California. Wish I could be in Los Angeles today!"

"You said it! Notre Dame is national champion—undefeated for two years. This year they've beaten Southern Methodist, Navy, Carnegie Tech, Pittsburgh, Indiana, Pennsylvania, Drake, Northwestern, and Army. That was a tough schedule!"

"But what about Southern California?" asked another. "They're the best in the West! And Notre Dame's two regular fullbacks are out of the game."

The first man cut in. "Rockne will come up with someone. He always does. Listen—there's the line-up—— He's starting Bucky O'Connor at fullback."

"Never heard of him."

"Well, before this day is over, you will."

"Maybe. Rockne usually has some surprise up his sleeve."

The men all chuckled. "Everybody tries to follow the Notre Dame system," said one, "but Rockne always keeps one jump ahead!"

"He even teaches the system to other coaches. He holds a school for them every year. And still they can't beat him."

The Notre Dame man said thoughtfully, "He's a fellow who really loves football. He believes in the game just as he believes in the university. And he has come to believe just as strongly in the Catholic faith. You know, he joined the Church a few years ago."

The other men nodded. "He makes a great contribution to Notre Dame in every way," said one.

"What do you think of his idea of sending a whole new team into a game instead of just one or two substitutes?" another man asked.

"Well, it certainly frightens the opposition. But there are other reasons, too."

"What do you mean?"

"Why, all the boys want to play, and Rockne likes to give them all a chance. Besides, he thinks he gets better teamwork that way."

Somebody turned up the radio. "The game's starting!"

As the men listened, they heard Notre Dame play one of its greatest games. Every player was performing at his best. Frank Carideo, All-American quarterback, had a fine day. A big star was Bucky O'Connor, the substitute full-back.

"What did I tell you?" said the man who had spoken of O'Connor. "What a game! 27 to 0!"

"It's amazing. National champion again! That makes five undefeated seasons for Notre Dame under Rockne. I wonder just how many games they've won and lost under him."

"Here it is in the paper up to this game. Under Rockne, Notre Dame has now played 122 games.

Counting today, they've won 105, lost twelve, and tied five. Rockne will surely go down in history as one of the greatest coaches of all time."

Out in California, someone was asking Knute, "Mr. Rockne, don't you think too much is being made of football, with these huge crowds and big stadiums?"

"No! Why shouldn't a lot of people enjoy football? It's a great game, and it's good for the boys."

He went on, very seriously: "I think football is a magnificent bodybuilder and character builder, too. It teaches boys to be rugged, exact, painstaking. It teaches them to stand up against life's hard blows."

He hesitated a moment. "Yes, I firmly believe that America's future battles, in peace and in war, are being won on the football gridirons of this country."

Back in Chicago, the men who had been listening tensely relaxed. One leaned forward to turn off the radio. "Well, Rockne's coached Notre Dame to four national championships now. 27 to 0! This team of 1930 is surely his finest."

"Rock himself will never say which he considers best. He just says they're all his boys, and he won't pick favorites."

"Even if his career were cut short now," put in another man, "Rockne would always be remembered as a great coach. And not just because of his amazing number of victories. He's a genius in his line—he has the gift of making his teams All-Americans in character as well as technique."

"Yes, he's raised the sport to the level of a science. Football's no longer only a show of physical strength."

"If ever there's a special Hall of Fame for football heroes, Knute Rockne will surely be the first coach included."

"He's had an influence on more than football. His ideals and sportsmanship have left their mark on all American athletics."